W9-BLD-385

THE FIVE ANCESTORS

鷹 Eagle

Jeff Stone

The Five Ancestors

Book 1: Tiger

Book 2: Monkey

Book 3: Snake

Book 4: Crane

Book 5: Eagle

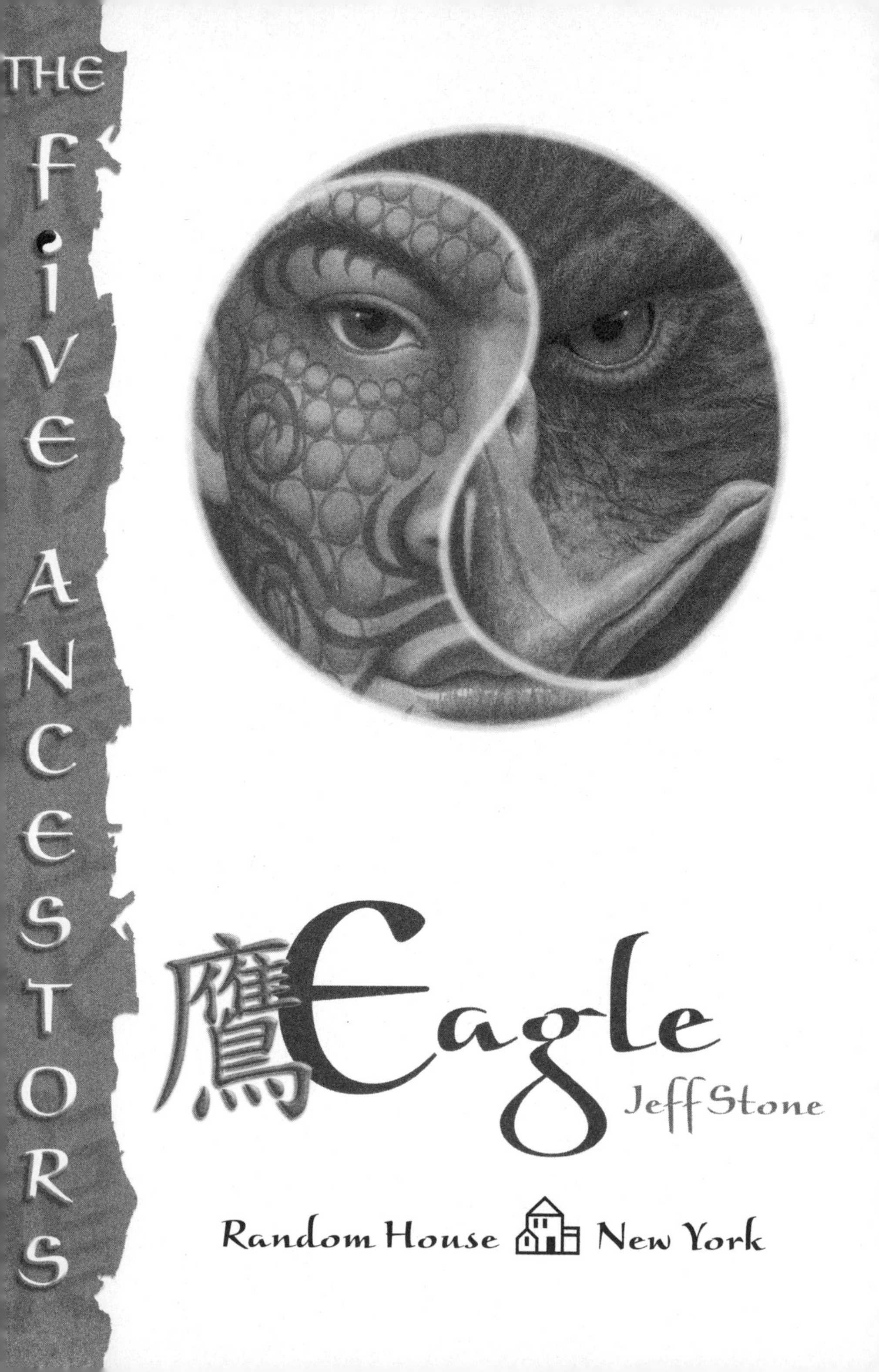

THE FIVE ANCESTORS

鷹 Eagle

Jeff Stone

Random House New York

Published in the United States by Random House Children's Books, a division of Random House, Inc., New York.

Random House and colophon are registered trademarks of Random House, Inc.

The Five Ancestors is a registered trademark of Jeffrey S. Stone.

Visit us on the Web! www.randomhouse.com/kids

Educators and librarians, for a variety of teaching tools, visit us at www.randomhouse.com/teachers

www.fiveancestors.com

Library of Congress Cataloging-in-Publication Data
Stone, Jeff.
Eagle / Jeff Stone. — 1st ed.
p. cm. — (The five ancestors ; bk. 5)
Summary: After attacking and killing his former grandmaster, sixteen-year-old Ying realizes he has been betrayed in addition to being wanted for treason, and consequently is forced to turn to Hok, his old temple sister, for help.
ISBN 978-0-375-83083-9 (trade) — ISBN 978-0-375-93083-6 (lib. bdg.) —
ISBN 978-0-375-83084-6 (pbk.)
[1. Martial arts—Fiction. 2. Human-animal relationships—Fiction. 3. Brothers and sisters—Fiction. 4. Revenge—Fiction. 5. Conduct of life—Fiction.] I. Title.
PZ7.S87783Eag 2008 [Fic]—dc22 2007049959

Printed in the United States of America
10 9 8 7 6 5 4 3 2 1
First Edition

for my father, Roger

THE FIVE ANCESTORS

鷹 Eagle

Jeff Stone

PROLOGUE

There is a legend told in warrior circles. One as old as history itself. It concerns the affairs of the four mystical dragons who held the world upon their backs—the Wind Dragon, the Sea Dragon, the Celestial Dragon, and the Treasure Dragon. They had a problem.

Humans.

Mankind was spreading quickly across the vast landscape that was China, and the humans were not doing so in a peaceful manner. They were doing so with warfare. This was upsetting to the dragons. They called a meeting.

"Let me bring a great gale and blow these troublesome human creatures off the face of the earth," the Wind Dragon offered.

The Celestial Dragon, their leader, frowned and shook his mighty head. "No, too violent."

"I could unleash a torrent of waves to wash the humans into oblivion," the Sea Dragon suggested.

The Celestial Dragon's brow furrowed. "How is that better? Destruction only begets destruction. No."

The Treasure Dragon, the cleverest of the bunch, rubbed his long whiskers. "It seems to me the humans are slow learners. I have witnessed short bursts of peace, which they seem to enjoy, but then they go back to war. They need to be constantly reminded of the simplest things. I will create gifts for them that their leaders will proudly carry wherever they go. Gifts with the power and significance to unite them. Gifts they understand."

The Celestial Dragon's brow rose up. "Tell me more."

"I will give them weapons," the Treasure Dragon said. "Matching tools of war that will be a constant reminder of their need for peace. Only the mighty can speak convincingly of peace, so I will make the gifts strong. Unbeatable, yet unable to beat any of the others. I will retreat to my underground lair and cut identical swords from the finest jade. Then I will assemble a magnificent suit of armor consisting of nine hundred ninety-nine jade plates. I will pour my very essence into these gifts until the green jade turns as white as the pearl of wisdom we dragons carry beneath our chins."

"That is very noble of you," the Celestial Dragon said. "How many swords will you make?"

"As many as I need to," the Treasure Dragon replied. "How have the humans divided themselves?"

"They've separated into the Four Winds," the Wind Dragon replied. "There is the Eastern Warlord, the

Western Warlord, the Southern Warlord, and the Emperor in the North. The Emperor is supposed to be their leader, but he is not strong enough."

"I will make four swords, then," the Treasure Dragon said. "One each for the three warlords, and one for the Emperor, who will also receive the armor. The Emperor will be the leader of leaders. With the armor, his word will be final. These enchanted gifts will bring them together. There will be peace."

"There might be peace," the Sea Dragon said, "but worse problems than war will arise if the Emperor's heart is tainted. The current Emperor suffers from this affliction. You cannot bestow such a powerful gift upon him. It would be disastrous."

"Then we shall wait," the Treasure Dragon replied. "I will hide the gifts in one of my treasure hoards and devise a test for those that might be worthy."

"How will the humans learn of this test?" the Celestial Dragon asked.

"I will spread rumors among individuals with the most potential. Strong, brave people who are not afraid to fight. If any among them are also intelligent and compassionate, not to mention clever, they might find my clues. If they can locate the hoard, they can keep my jewels, as well as the swords and armor."

"You cannot spend all your time watching and waiting for a human who might never exist," the Sea Dragon said. "Your responsibilities are great."

"I will appoint a keeper," the Treasure Dragon said. "A watcher, of sorts. There must be one human out there

who is worthy of knowing my secret. Someone with a keen eye and a good heart. Someone who might not be a great leader but can see greatness in others. I will make this individual swear to keep the hoard's location secret within his or her family, for it may be many generations before someone worthy surfaces. As long as the family remains untainted, the treasure should never fall into the wrong hands."

The Celestial Dragon nodded. "Jade is like a mirror. It reflects and amplifies whatever is near. In the right hands, your swords will bring peace and unity as you intended, and over the right shoulders, the armor will ensure that the peace lasts. However, in the wrong hands, ill intentions will be magnified. There is risk, but your idea is sound. Make it so."

The Treasure Dragon bowed. He flexed his eagle talons and stood. "I had better get to work. I fear it will take me longer to find a keeper than it will to carve the swords. It seems the fate of mankind may rest in the character of a single individual. I had better choose wisely."

Henan Province, China
4348 – Year of the Tiger
(1650 AD)

CHAPTER 1

*B*ANG!

Sixteen-year-old Ying shoved his former sister, Hok, to the ground with all his might. He saw her eyes widen as a *qiang* ball whistled over her head. Ying's carved face twisted into an angry scowl. How many times was he going to have to save her life tonight? He turned and slammed the door closed on the burning arena of the Jinan Fight Club.

Inside the club's main tunnel, Ying's eyes quickly adjusted to the orange-yellow glow of torches lining the stone-walled corridor. He glanced down at Hok and, next to her, Seh. Through the smoke drifting in from under the door, Ying saw that Hok held a tiny jade crane in one hand and Malao's ornate monkey stick in the other. Both were trophies from her time in the pit arena.

In his own hands, Ying held his long chain whip and a ring of keys he'd just taken from LaoShu, the *qiang*-wielding fight club owner.

LaoShu screamed suddenly on the other side of the door, and Ying heard roof timbers crash down. The ground and walls shook, and Ying knew that LaoShu—the *Rat*—would give them no more trouble.

Ying spat and pivoted away from the door, ignoring the pain of cracked ribs and weeks-old bone bruises. The nagging injuries were *his* trophies, presented to him in prison by General Tsung almost a month before.

Ying wrapped his chain whip around his waist and groaned. He grabbed the collar of Hok's dress, yanking her to her feet.

"Move!" Ying hissed, pointing down the corridor. He looked at his former brother Seh. "You too."

Hok took a step forward, but Seh didn't react. He just stared at Ying, blank-faced.

What is wrong with Seh? Ying wondered. He reached out to slap some sense into him, but Hok grabbed his arm.

"Seh is blind," Hok said. "Not deaf. He had an accident."

"Blind?" Ying said. "Leave him, then."

Hok shook her head. "No."

Ying shrugged. "Suit yourself." He spun around and walked quickly down the tunnel corridor, the rough cotton robe of his Pit Cleaner disguise chafing his beaten flesh.

"Ying, wait," Hok said. She took Seh by the arm and hurried after Ying.

Ying slowed for a moment, scanning the corridor. He saw no sign of guards ahead. They must have cleared out after the fire began.

Ying glanced back and saw Hok and Seh catching up. They looked like a pair of children whose dress-up tea party had ended in a fistfight. Hok's elegant silk dress was torn in several places and bloodstained from her fierce battle with General Tsung in the pit arena. Seh's simple gray robe was covered in dirt and splotches of who knows what else from rolling along the pit-arena floor en route to this tunnel.

Ying began to walk again. Hok and Seh remained on his tail.

"Why are you helping us?" Hok soon asked in a low voice.

"You got me out of that prison back in Kaifeng," Ying replied. "I am returning the favor."

"You already met your end of our bargain," Hok said. "You gave me information that helped me find Malao."

Ying scoffed. "Maybe you would consider information an equal trade for someone's life, but I do not. My injuries were too great for me to have survived much longer there. You saved my life, and I am honor-bound to return the favor."

"But how did you know we would be here in Jinan, at the fight club?" Hok asked.

"I didn't come to Jinan looking for you," Ying replied. "I came looking for Tonglong. I have a score to settle with him, and he frequents the fight clubs. I saw you and Seh standing in line outside with the round eye. I assumed you were up to something, and also assumed you would fail. I saw this as an opportunity to repay my debt."

Ying rounded a corner. Ahead of him were rows of holding cells for prisoners who were scheduled to fight that night. All of the cells were empty save two. Inside one sat Fu. Malao was in the other.

Fu roared when he saw Ying, but Malao began to shriek, "Ying! Ying!"

One of Malao's shoulders was bloodstained, and he had a huge lump on the side of his head.

Ying ignored him.

"What are you doing here?" Malao asked. "Are those *keys* in your hand?"

Ying hurried past without acknowledging him. He picked up his pace.

"Ying, wait!" Malao wailed. "Come back!"

Ying glanced over his shoulder and saw Hok heading toward the cells with Seh.

"Hok! Hok!" Malao shrieked. "Help us!"

Fu roared again.

"Ying!" Hok said. "Please come back. Malao is hurt. We need those keys."

"Sorry," Ying said, turning away. "I need the keys for the exit door."

"Let them out first," Hok said.

“No,” Ying said. “There are too many keys on this ring. By the time I figure out which ones will open their cells, we could be dead from smoke or something else. I won’t risk it.”

“I am not leaving here without Fu and Malao,” Hok said.

“Then my debt has been repaid,” Ying said. “Goodbye.”

Ying rounded another corner and began to run. *Foolish children,* he thought. *Don’t know when to cut their losses.*

Ying reached the end of the next passageway and came to a halt. The tunnel split in two directions. One way led to a set of stairs that went up to the fight club, while the other corridor sloped gently upward toward a ground-level exit door. If he were to encounter any guards or others fleeing the burning fight club, this would be the place.

Ying squeezed the key ring tight so it wouldn’t jingle and peered around the corner. Smoke was streaming toward the exit. That meant the exit door was open, sucking the smoke toward it.

Ying listened closely.

Down the corridor in the direction of the exit, he heard footsteps. Someone coughed. “I can’t believe we’re being sent back in here,” a man said. “We should just wait by the exit door. It’s the only way out for those kids.”

“I don’t make the orders,” another man replied. “I only follow them. The captain said to make a quick sweep of the tunnels, then get out of here. The sooner we finish, the sooner we can get some fresh air. Men, prepare your *qiangs*."

Ying noted the unmistakable *click* of a *qiang* mechanism being engaged, then another, and another. He might be able to get past a single soldier with a *qiang*, but not three. Especially in his weakened state. Unfortunately, he needed help.

Ying silently ran back toward the others, cursing his terrible luck. As he neared the cells, he could hear Malao sobbing. He also heard Fu pounding furiously against the bars.

Hok saw Ying first. She opened her mouth to speak, but Ying cut her off. "There are at least three men coming this way with *qiangs*," he said. "They intend to finish us. If I release Fu and Malao, will you follow my orders?"

Fu growled, but Malao said, "I'll do it, Ying! I'll do whatever you say! I'm a little dizzy and my shoulder is sore, but I can still fight. Get me out of here!"

"Hush!" Ying said. "Keep your voice down." He stared hard at Fu. "What about you, Pussycat?"

Fu didn't reply.

Hok gave Fu an icy stare. "Be logical, Fu," she said. "There isn't much time."

"Fine," Fu grumbled, locking eyes with Ying.

Ying fought back a smirk. Fu was irritating and immature, but at least he was always ready for a fight. Fu would go first.

Ying flipped through the ring of keys, selected one,

and stuck it into Malao's cell door. The door swung open.

"Hey!" Malao whined. "You said you didn't know which key would open this door."

"Lucky guess," Ying snapped. He walked over to Fu's cell and unlocked it. As the door swung open, Fu snarled in Ying's face and muscled past.

"After you, Pussycat," Ying said. "Put those feline instincts to use."

Fu rushed forward.

Ying started after Fu, and Hok handed the monkey stick to Malao. Malao grinned excitedly. "Where did you get this?"

"From HaMo while I was inside the fight club," Hok replied. "I'll tell you about it later. Are you sure you're okay?"

"I'm fine," Malao said. He and Hok followed, with Seh in between them.

Fu soon stopped, and Ying watched Fu's head tilt to one side. Fu's low-light eyesight was excellent, but his ears were even better. Fu sank to his haunches and held up four fingers.

Four guards, Ying thought. *That's five against four. No problem.* He looked back at Hok, Seh, and Malao and held up four fingers. Hok and Malao nodded back. Hok whispered the information into Seh's ear.

Ying sank to the ground and slipped the chain whip from around his waist. He gathered it up in one hand, shoving the key ring behind his sash. He slid over to Fu's side and mouthed five words: *Angry Tiger Moves the Mountain.*

Fu nodded once and compressed his body into a large ball. A heavy boot scraped the floor just ahead of them, and Fu sprang with a tremendous roar.

"Oooof!" the lead guard groaned as Fu slammed into his midsection. The guard's long *qiang* fired on impact with a characteristic *click . . . fizz . . . BANG!*, the lead ball burying itself harmlessly in the wall of the tunnel. Fu hammered a tiger-claw fist into the man's jaw, silencing him.

"What's going on up there?" a guard called out.

No one offered a reply.

Ying eased his back against the tunnel's stone wall and saw the outline of a second guard creeping forward with his long *qiang* leveled at Fu's head.

"Crazy Monkey Swats the Fly!" Ying shouted, and Malao responded by racing forward, swinging his monkey stick wildly. The guard saw Malao coming and shifted his arms to protect himself, but he was too slow. Malao leaped high into the air and brought the monkey stick down on the crown of the man's skull with a tremendous crack. The guard slumped to the ground, out cold, his finger still on the *qiang*'s trigger.

Click . . . fizz . . . BANG!

The *qiang* fired, its fire stone–tipped hammer igniting black powder. The lead ball shot forward, and the unsupported weapon flew backward out of the unconscious man's hands. The *qiang* crashed against one wall of the tunnel, while the lead ball thudded into the opposite tunnel wall in a shower of debris.

Two down, two to go, Ying thought.

A third guard stepped up through thickening smoke and froze at the sight of his unconscious comrades being stood over by two children. Ying took advantage of the man's hesitation and lashed out with his chain whip. The whip's weighted end wrapped itself around the end of the guard's *qiang* several times. Ying yanked the barrel of the *qiang* down and sideways, and shouted, "Monkey Takes the High Road, Tiger Takes the Low!"

Fu and Malao attacked as one. Fu threw his shoulders into the man's knees at the same moment Malao sprang into the air and slammed his heels into the man's cheekbones. The guard sailed backward, releasing his grip on the *qiang* in order to use his hands to break his fall. That proved to be unnecessary, as the fourth guard ended up breaking the third guard's fall for him.

Fu wrestled the *qiang* from the fourth guard's hands, and Malao put both guards to sleep with his monkey stick.

Ying unwrapped his chain whip from the end of the third guard's *qiang* and put the whip back around his waist. He pointed to the remaining unfired *qiang* Fu was holding and said, "Give that to me."

Fu growled and took a step back.

Hok gave Fu a cold glance. "Do it, Fu," she said.

Fu handed the *qiang* over.

Ying slung one of the *qiangs* over his shoulder and pulled the second one tight across his chest.

"Follow me," Ying hissed. "No matter what happens, do not stop walking."

"What are we going to—" Malao began.

"No questions!" Ying snapped. He turned and walked away. Behind him, he heard the others scramble and follow.

When Ying reached the bend where he'd first heard the guards, he turned the corner without breaking stride. The smoke was quite thick now, still flowing toward the exit door. Perfect. The exit door was still open. He would no longer need the keys.

Ying stopped and laid the key ring down, then quickly looked over the *qiangs*. The pans were full of powder, and the flints were locked firmly in place at the ends of the hammers. He could only hope that each had a lead ball rammed down its barrel.

Ying slung one of the *qiangs* across his back, raised the other to his shoulder, and headed for the exit door.

CHAPTER 2

Ying strode through the tunnel exit door with all the confidence of a seasoned general, smoke wafting around him in the hot night air. Three guards stood in a cluster fifteen paces from him in a narrow alley behind the burning fight club.

The men stopped in mid-conversation and stared for several moments through the darkness before one of them had the sense to try to raise his *qiang*.

"Put that down!" Ying barked, swinging his own *qiang* toward the man. "All of you, lay your weapons on the ground!" Ying fanned his *qiang* back and forth between the guards. The first guard lowered his weapon. The others followed suit.

Ying continued forward, making eye contact with

each of the men. They were young, not much older than him, and probably unseasoned. He bared his pointed teeth and flicked out his forked tongue in the dim firelight. All three men flinched.

Definitely unseasoned, Ying thought. He knew that any two of them could have raised their *qiang*s and fired, and he would certainly have fallen. However, one of them would most certainly have fallen, too. None of them was willing to take that chance.

"Lie down!" Ying spat.

The guards looked tentatively at one another. One of them glanced toward the exit doorway. "Look!" he said. "It's the girl from the pit arena—"

"Quiet!" Ying hissed, his finger on his *qiang*'s trigger.

The man closed his mouth. Ying nodded at the cobblestones, and the guard dropped to the ground. Ying fanned his *qiang* across the other guards again, and they dropped to the ground, too.

"Fu! Malao!" Ying snapped. "Pick up the *qiang*s."

Malao scampered through the doorway and grabbed a *qiang* that was longer than he was tall. Fu grabbed the other two.

"Let's go," Ying said. "Hok, lead the way."

Hok stepped around Ying, holding Seh's hand. Seh's arm brushed against Ying's elbow, and Ying felt something move beneath Seh's sleeve. A snake?

Ying smacked his lips. He could use some fresh snake blood. But not right now.

"Count to one hundred before you even think about getting up," Ying said to the guards.

The guards began to count quietly, "*Yi* . . . *er* . . . *san* . . ."

Ying backed away quickly, staying close to the others. As they neared the point where the alley met the main road, Hok asked, "Which way?"

"Left," Ying replied. "Then we will make a quick right and another right. We aren't going far."

They stepped out of the alley into pure pandemonium. People were racing back and forth along a wide street that skirted the burning fight club. Everyone was carrying armloads of items out of the surrounding buildings in case the fire spread.

Ying knew they would be safe in this melee. He lowered his *qiang* and let Hok continue to lead as he kept watch across their flank. He spotted no one suspicious, and no one took notice of them. As far as anyone was concerned, they, too, were simply fleeing the flames with valuables.

They soon reached the spot Ying had in mind. It was a narrow alleyway slick with slime and reeking of open sewer. It was approximately forty paces long and five paces wide, with a three-story building surrounding it on three sides. Stained windowsills dotted the buildings from top to bottom. All the windows were closed tight to ward off the stench of human waste and other filth that was regularly tossed out of them.

"What is this place?" Hok asked.

"Home," Ying replied.

"You *live* here?" Malao said, plugging his nose. He lifted one of his bare feet and wiggled his toes. "This place makes my feet smell as sweet as water lilies! Yuck! Why would *anybody* live here?"

"Exactly," Ying said. "Now, lean the *qiang*s against a wall and leave."

Malao gave Hok a questioning look.

"Do as he says," Hok said. "We need to be on our way. We still have much work to do."

"Work?" Malao asked, leaning his *qiang* against a wall.

"We have to find someone," Hok replied. "His name is Charles."

Fu leaned his *qiang*s next to Malao's and growled, "Not the round eye?"

Hok nodded. "Yes, the Dutch boy."

"Why would you help a foreigner?" Ying asked as he gathered up the three *qiang*s plus the two he carried and headed for a back corner of the alley. He placed the *qiang*s beneath a large flea-ridden blanket.

"Charles is my friend," Hok said matter-of-factly. "Friends help each other."

Ying scoffed. "A foreigner as a friend? They are nothing but trouble."

"You wouldn't understand anything about friendship," Fu said. "We all know what you did to your only friend, Luk—"

Ying spat and turned toward Fu. "How *dare* you say that?"

Fu shrugged.

"Do not disrespect me, Pussycat," Ying said, walking toward Fu. "Do not disrespect Luk's memory, either."

Seh stepped in front of Fu, his blind eyes seeking Fu's face. Ying saw the snake beneath Seh's robe begin to quiver.

"That's enough, Fu," Seh said. "We will leave now."

"Yes," Hok added, stepping forward and placing her hands on Fu's shoulders. "We all know what happened to Luk was an accident. Let us leave."

"It was not an accident," Fu growled.

Ying felt his heart rate begin to rise. "Are you looking for a fight, Pussycat?" Ying asked. "If so, you've come to the right place."

Seh turned toward Ying and put his hands up as if to ward him off. Ying walked straight into them, pressing his chest against Seh's palms. "Would you like to dance with me, too, Seh?"

"I'm not afraid of you," Seh replied. "But I'm not looking for a fight, if that is what you mean."

Ying glanced at the snake outlined beneath Seh's sleeve. It was moving toward Seh's wrist. It had been a long time since Ying had savored fresh snake blood. He smacked his lips and reached for Seh's arm.

A slender blue and black head lashed out from Seh's sleeve. Ying stepped backward, pulling his right hand out of the way while swinging his left hand forward in an eagle-claw fist. He had caught many snakes this way.

Seh must have sensed Ying's movements because he twisted around, jerking his arm and the snake out of Ying's reach. Ying's left hand continued forward, connecting with the small of Seh's back.

Seh lunged away from Ying, but Ying grabbed hold

of Seh's sash. The sash came loose, and something tumbled to the ground from beneath Seh's robe. Ying glanced down and his eyes widened. It was a scroll.

Ying dove toward the scroll like a bird of prey after a garden snake, but a tiny hand got there first.

Malao let out a screech and leaped at one of the walls, out of Ying's reach, the scroll in one hand. Ying watched Malao grip a stained windowsill with his free hand and hoist himself up, then spring from windowsill to windowsill, higher and higher, until he was on the roof of the building.

Malao looked down at Ying and giggled, waving the scroll over his head. Blood trickled from the wound in his shoulder, but he didn't seem to notice.

Hok stared coldly at Ying. "Do not try that again. If you attempt another attack, you will face all of us."

Ying hissed. He pointed up at Malao. "Is that a dragon scroll?"

Fu took a step toward Ying. "What if it is?"

"Then it belongs to me," Ying replied. "Hand it over."

"Why don't you fly up there and get it yourself?" Fu challenged. "Or did somebody clip your wings recently? That attack was pitiful."

Ying snarled, and Hok stepped between him and Fu. Ying locked eyes with Hok. "What do you think you are doing?"

"Keeping peace," Hok said. She glanced up at Malao, then back at Ying. "I have a proposition. You know as well as I do that you'll never catch Malao, even if he is injured. I might be willing to show you that scroll, though, if you agree to help us find my friend Charles."

"Show it to me?" Ying said. He shook his head. "You will give it to me."

"I can't do that," Hok replied. "It's not mine to give. However, a few moments with the scroll will be enough to satisfy you. I know how intensely you've trained in the ways of memory enhancement."

"I am good," Ying said. "But not that good. No one is. The one dragon scroll I do have took days to commit to memory."

"This one is different," Hok said. "It's much simpler."

"How simple?"

"It is a map."

Ying blinked. "A map?"

"Why are you telling him this?" Seh asked.

"Because we need his help," Hok replied.

"We don't need it that bad," Seh said.

"I believe we do," Hok said.

Ying stared at both of them, then at Fu, and finally up at Malao. It was clear that none of them had any idea where the map led. If they did, they would never have told another soul. Least of all, him.

Hok looked at Ying. "I can tell by your reaction that you are interested. Do we have a deal?"

Ying paused and a drop of water fell onto his nose. He glanced up into the night sky and several more pelted his carved face. It was beginning to rain.

Seh cleared his throat. "We need to take cover. I sense this rain will be heavy."

Ying looked over at Malao again, a tiny figure fidgeting on the rooftop. Hok was right. He would never catch Malao, especially in his own weakened state.

Ying nodded to Hok. "We have a deal."

Hok wiped rain from her brow. "Then it is agreed. I propose we meet at the wharf in two days' time. There is a small, well-cared-for skiff docked alongside the large seafaring vessels in the central section of docks. It is clearly visible from the main street. I will meet you there just after sunset. I will wear a disguise."

"Show me the map first," Ying said.

"No. We can finalize the details when we next meet."

Ying was about to argue when he heard Malao scurrying about the rooftop. Malao called down in a whisper, "Soldiers are coming!"

Ying frowned at Hok. "Get out. I'll see you in two days. Turn right out of this alley and follow the street for several *li.* It leads to the river."

Hok nodded and signaled to Malao to follow her from above. She disappeared into the gloom with Seh on her arm and Fu at her side.

Ying hurried over to the corner where he'd placed the *qiang*s and sank down, taking a deep breath of stagnant, sewer-fumed air. He stifled a cough and pulled the wet, tattered blanket over himself and the *qiang*s, then closed his eyes.

Ying was confident that he wouldn't be found in

this dismal location. He was even more confident that he would not get what he needed most—sleep. Between the talk of memorizing a map and the mention of Luk, Ying knew sleep would be impossible.

It seemed sleepless nights were the price he would forever pay for mastering the one thing that only he and Grandmaster had ever managed to master: memory intensification. It was a powerful skill, but with it came a great burden.

The trouble with remembering everything was that you never forgot anything. Even if you wanted to.

CHAPTER 3

Ying was fourteen years old when his best friend, Luk, died. Killed by a *qiang* as Ying stood and watched. Ying seemed doomed to replay the scene over and over in his mind, trying to determine if he might have done something differently. The memories were especially vivid after smelling the smoke from a freshly fired *qiang,* or after someone had mentioned Luk's name. Tonight, Ying had experienced both. He knew he would never be able to dam the flood of images, so he let them flow.

The mission was supposed to be simple. Sneak into a house while the owner was away and retrieve some documents. Simple enough for fourteen-year-old Ying and his fifteen-year-old best friend, Luk, to handle while a group of warrior monks waited more than a *li* away.

Ying had memorized the home's floor plan. He knew exactly where to go. Luk was there to kick down locked doors with his mighty back-kick, perfected by a lifetime of deer-style kung fu training.

Simple.

However, Grandmaster's information had been flawed. The house wasn't empty.

Ying had never seen anything like the object the home's owner was holding when Luk kicked down the first door. It was a long metal tube partially wrapped in wood, braced tightly against the man's shoulder. He would never forget the terrific *BANG!* accompanied by a burst of flame and a huge cloud of smoke. Luk falling to the ground with a large hole in his side.

Grandmaster should have warned them about the *qiangs*. He should have warned them about a lot of things. But he never did, because this was his way.

Ying still completed the mission, personally handing the documents to the Emperor. The Emperor asked what had happened to Luk, and Ying found he could do little more than shrug. When the Emperor asked what had happened to the homeowner, Ying showed the Emperor the bits of flesh wedged beneath his fingernails and the bloodstains on his robe. No further explanation was needed. The Emperor patted Ying on the back and told him if he ever wanted to leave Cangzhen and make a name for himself, Ying should contact one of his palaces. Ying said he just might.

When Ying returned to Cangzhen, everyone acted as if nothing had happened. Luk was no longer with them in the dining hall or the practice hall or the sleeping quarters, but life continued as usual. Ying could hardly control his rage. The only person he cared about, the only person he trusted, was gone.

No one understood Ying's friendship with Luk, the aggressive eagle and the timid deer. But it made perfect sense to Ying. They were *yin* and *yang*. Opposites that balanced one another out. Luk had helped Ying calm down whenever he became angry, while Ying had taught Luk to stand up for himself. Even so, Luk had never actually hurt anybody. Not even a mosquito. Luk should never have been part of the mission in the first place.

Ying complained to the senior monks, but they didn't listen. The more questions he asked, the more they turned their backs to him.

Ying realized that he was nothing more than a tool. Just another weapon in Grandmaster's growing arsenal. The more he thought about it, the more Ying realized that he and the other Cangzhen monks were simply muscle to be flexed at Grandmaster's whim. Grandmaster had been making Ying's life miserable as far back as he could remember, and for what? To make Ying a better person? No. Grandmaster had been doing it to serve his own interests.

Grandmaster had been responsible for sending Luk to his death. Grandmaster had also killed Ying's father in front of him when he was just a toddler and had driven his mother away. Grandmaster had taken Ying to Cangzhen, changed his name, and raised him to be something he wasn't, all in an effort to make Cangzhen stronger.

Ying's rage intensified. Grandmaster had stripped him of his identity. He'd taken away the few people Ying had ever been close to. Grandmaster had ruined Ying's life, leaving him with nothing. Not even a sense of who he was, or who he was supposed to be. Ying would never forget Luk's final words, "Goodbye, Saulong. I hope you find yourself. I hope you learn to trust another."

Ying knew he would never trust another soul, but he was determined to find himself, even if it meant looking under the body of every man in China.

Ying went to see the Emperor.

The Emperor sent Ying to the fight clubs, where Ying thrived. Ying had felt invisible at Cangzhen, but in the fight clubs he quickly made a name for himself. Still, it wasn't enough. He wanted to be respected. He wanted to be feared.

In a city called Xuzhou, there was a foreign fighter from a faraway island. The man had deep grooves carved into his cheeks, nose, and forehead, and the grooves were tinted a deep green. He looked menacing, and his looks earned him instant respect. Ying decided he wanted the same thing. He asked the foreigner to carve his face, but the foreigner laughed at him. He told Ying that the facial carving was for true warriors only.

Ying attacked the man on the spot, breaking both the foreigner's hands in quick succession. Needless to say, the man didn't fight again for quite some time. Once his hands healed, he did as Ying asked.

The foreigner told Ying that the lines he would carve would be dictated by Ying's inner spirit, and that no one could predict how it would turn out. After two days of excruciating carving and pigmenting—and a month of healing—the final result surprised the foreigner, but not Ying. Ying had been transformed into the dragon he always knew he was. He took his new identity a step further, sharpening his teeth and forking and elongating his tongue. For the first time, people saw his true self. And they ran. Ying loved it.

Ying went on to win the Fight Club Championship and was appointed a major within the Emperor's ranks. His face was a powerful tool, striking fear into the hearts of the men he fought in the arenas and into the souls of the young men he commanded. Ying would simply curl back his lips, and his soldiers would jump over the moon if he told them to. They even took his direction on a suicide mission against Cangzhen Temple, where two thousand of his men went in and only two hundred came out. Several weeks later, he sent his remaining men on another suicide mission against the stronghold of the region's most powerful bandits. All he had had to do was scowl, and they had obeyed.

However, now that Tonglong had betrayed him and he was officially an escaped prisoner, Ying's face was a burden. He could no longer show it. Leave it to Tonglong to twist Ying's successes at Cangzhen and the bandit stronghold so that the Emperor would lock him in prison. Apparently, fear was not the only tool a person could use to accomplish his objectives. Tonglong had used strategy. Tonglong's plans had unfolded so slowly, Ying had been oblivious to them. Ying would never fall for such subtle trickery again.

Ying took another deep breath of putrid air beneath the wet blanket and popped his knuckles, one at a time. He had already taken care of Grandmaster. Next on his list was Tonglong.

CHAPTER 4

Ying spent most of the following day beneath the wet, tattered blanket, only lifting one corner a few times to drink from the heavy rain that continued to fall. He was soaked to the bone and hungry, but there was little he could do about it. He had shown his face and men would be looking for him, especially in the daylight.

The clouds broke just before sunset, the rain softening to a fine mist. Not ideal conditions, but they would have to do. It was time for the hunted to become the hunter.

Ying peeled back the rotting blanket and squeezed dirty rainwater from his short black hair. The foul liquid coursed through the grooves in his carved cheeks, dripping down onto his Pit Cleaner's uniform. He made a mental note to get new clothes soon.

Ying tore a section of the blanket loose and tied it around his head and face, like a leper, leaving only his eyes showing. The cloth reeked of mold. He stifled a cough and looked at the *qiang*s beside him.

Foreigners' weapons, Ying thought. *Weapons for the weak.*

All five *qiang*s were slightly different in appearance but worked the same way. Ying had learned about them while serving the Emperor. The user pulled a metal hammer back with his thumb until the hammer locked in place. The hammer was fitted with a small piece of fire stone, and when a trigger beneath the *qiang* was pulled, the hammer released, causing the fire stone to swing forward and strike a metal plate. The fire stone would release a spray of sparks. Most times, one of the sparks would drop through a small hole into a pan that contained explosive black powder. The powder would ignite, in turn igniting a larger quantity of black powder that had been loaded directly into the *qiang* barrel behind a ball of lead. The resulting explosion would propel the lead ball out of the *qiang*'s barrel at amazing speed.

Ying knew that Chinese had invented black powder hundreds of years earlier, but it was mostly used for fireworks at celebrations. It was foreigners who had taken black powder and developed these weapons.

Foreign *qiang*s came in many shapes and sizes, from the size of a person's hand to huge "cannons" that shot iron balls the size of a man's head. Ying knew this firsthand, as it was only through the power of *qiangs* that he was able to destroy Cangzhen Temple with his army of young, unseasoned soldiers. It was a test of the *qiangs*' capabilities, the Emperor had said, and the results were undeniable. The *qiangs* had done the job better than Ying or anyone else could ever have imagined. Ying had even used a short *qiang* hidden up his sleeve to take care of Grandmaster.

Even so, Ying disliked *qiangs*. Using one took little skill and even less honor. Any monkey could fire a *qiang*. He saw them only as a weapon of last resort, nothing at all like the chain whip he wore around his waist. The chain whip was intimate. Using it required you to be close enough to look your opponent in the eye. It was his favorite. However, what he needed to do now required distance.

Ying ran his hand over each *qiang*, selecting three that had covers to protect their firing mechanisms from the weather. He would leave the other two behind.

Ying wrung out the blanket, wrapped up the three choice *qiangs*, and headed out of the alley.

CHAPTER 5

Tonglong stood in the waning daylight, surveying the remains of the Jinan Fight Club. He was surprised by how quickly it had been reduced to rubble.

The building had collapsed upon itself during the fire, leaving little more than a tiered ring of stone walls around the deep pit arena. Fortunately for the city of Jinan, only a few sections of the surrounding buildings had burned, thanks to the heavy rains. Now that the rain had finally stopped, twenty men were in the pit, methodically sifting through charred roof timbers and other rain-soaked debris. Fifty more men combed the fight club's vast network of tunnels, searching for clues to where the children and Ying might have fled.

Tonglong adjusted his long ponytail braid over his

shoulder and watched the recovery operation. In all, he had roughly one hundred soldiers in his charge, plus a handful of individuals who had worked as employees of the fight club. The men varied in age, but most of his soldiers were young, age sixteen or seventeen. This was typical. At twenty-nine, Tonglong was considered an old-timer. His men looked up to him, which was a far cry from how they had felt about their former leader, Ying.

Foolish, arrogant boy, Tonglong thought with a smile. Ying had been in a unique position. He had entered the fight clubs at age fifteen and been crowned champion before he'd turned sixteen. Also, Ying was from this region and therefore eligible to serve the Emperor by leading a small army.

Tonglong was nearly twice as old as Ying, and he was a former Fight Club Grand Champion, too. However, Tonglong had never been allowed to lead a large force. He was from a region in the south of China, and the Emperor, a northerner, considered him a foreigner.

Tonglong yearned to become a general, and he had realized that if he could get close to Ying, he might have a chance at realizing his goal. If he could position himself as Ying's right-hand man and then arrange a situation in which Ying would fail the Emperor, the Emperor might just give Tonglong Ying's troops. And that's exactly what happened.

The men now under Tonglong's charge weren't very skilled, but they were loyal. Tonglong was doing what he could to whip them into shape quickly, and they seemed to embrace his rigorous training. To them, anything was better than Ying's constant selfish demands. Ying was clever, but he was too consumed with revenge to see beyond his immediate target. He would have sacrificed every one of his soldiers to accomplish his goals, and his men knew it. They hated Ying for it.

What a waste of talent, Tonglong thought. Ying was now an enemy, and he would not live to see his seventeenth birthday. Tonglong would see to that personally.

In the meantime, Tonglong would continue with the next phase of his plan—getting close to the Emperor. This was coming along nicely, thanks to his mother's charms. There was also the matter of the dragon scroll map that the children from Cangzhen possessed. If the legends were true, its secret would allow Tonglong to rise to power far sooner than he could ever have imagined. In many ways, finding the children was more critical than finding Ying.

Tonglong frowned. In the past, he had made the mistake of allowing the children to gain possession of several dragon kung fu training scrolls. He had done this to keep the scrolls out of Ying's hands. Unfortunately, Tonglong had incorrectly assumed that he could find the children and take the scrolls back at a moment's notice. He would never underestimate those children again.

Tonglong wiped his sweaty brow and scanned the soldiers in the pit arena below. They needed to find something soon, before the trail grew too cold. He glanced over at the remnants of the large wooden door that had separated the pit arena from the main tunnel. This was the last place he'd seen Ying and the children. All that was left was a gaping black hole in the pit-arena wall. Soldiers should be coming back out of it anytime now with updated intelligence.

"General Tonglong!" a voice called from the pit. "Over here, sir, if you please."

Tonglong stared down his nose at one of the fight-club employees, a young man called GumLong, or *Golden Dragon* in Cantonese. Golden Dragon was the fight club owner's number one assistant, and he was making quite a name for himself fighting in the pit arenas. Not since Ying had someone caused such a commotion. Rumor had it that he was only fifteen years old, as Ying had been.

"What is it, Golden Dragon?" Tonglong asked.

"I've found something, sir," Golden Dragon replied. "I believe it is the remains of LaoShu, the fight club owner."

Tonglong noted the boy's steady voice. He didn't seem the least bit shaken by what he was looking at. Most people would be horrified if they'd uncovered any sort of human remains, let alone their boss's.

Tonglong leaned over the pit, eyeing Golden Dragon carefully. Regardless of the boy's age, he acted like a grown man. He was mature, wise, and well mannered. He reminded Tonglong of himself.

Golden Dragon swept aside a layer of wet soot

and lifted something from the muck. Tonglong saw a charred human hand. A gaudy gold ring was fused to one finger, and atop the ring sat a large jade rat. The ring was so large, Tonglong could easily see it from where he stood.

Tonglong nodded. "LaoShu, indeed. Well done."

Golden Dragon nodded back, then turned to the pit entrance tunnel.

Tonglong looked down at the huge doorway and saw one of his soldiers step through it, along with one of the fight club employees. Between them was a prisoner. The prisoner's wrists and ankles were bound with short lengths of rope, but it was obvious they weren't necessary. The man could barely hold himself up. His face and robes were black with soot, and his sallow skin hung from his cheeks like dry parchment. He moaned, "Water, please. . . ."

"Where did you find him?" Tonglong asked.

"In the farthest tunnel reserved for fight club participants," the soldier replied.

Tonglong paused. "Isn't that the tunnel where the round eye was being held?"

"Yes, sir," the fight club employee replied. "After he was apprehended at the bettors' table, we placed the round eye in one of the cells there. We should have him out momentarily."

"Nice work, men," Tonglong said. He turned back to Golden Dragon, who was staring up out of the pit, into the distance.

Tonglong raised his eyes to the numerous three-

and four-story buildings surrounding them. Most were apartment buildings with shops on the ground floor. There was also the city's main temple, immediately to the west. This was the direction in which Golden Dragon was looking.

Tonglong turned toward the temple and stared into the setting sun. At first, he saw nothing but glare, but then three figures stepped out of the temple, into the street. One person was quite small, one was of average size, and one was gigantic. Golden Dragon had sensed them somehow.

Tonglong gripped the hilt of his straight sword, then relaxed as the figures came nearer. The giant was Xie, or *Scorpion,* the Emperor's personal bodyguard, while the medium-sized figure was the Emperor himself.

Tonglong had to stifle a grin when he saw the small person. It was a beautiful middle-aged woman with long, luxurious hair. One of her arms was coiled around the Emperor's arm in an affectionate embrace. It was Tonglong's mother, AnGangseh.

Tonglong bowed low when the trio approached. "Greetings, Your Highness," he said.

The Emperor sniffed. "What do you have to report?"

Tonglong straightened. "We've found LaoShu's remains," he replied proudly.

"Are you certain it is him?" the Emperor asked.

"Positive."

The Emperor scratched his nose. "I see." He glanced into the pit at Golden Dragon, who was kneeling, his forehead poised just above the muck.

“You look familiar, boy,” the Emperor said. “Have we met?”

Golden Dragon shook his head. “No, Your Highness. I have not had the honor.”

“I am sure I’ve seen you before . . . ,” the Emperor muttered. He turned and ran his fingers through AnGangseh’s thick black hair.

“His name is Golden Dragon,” AnGangseh purred.

“Of course!” the Emperor said. “I am pleased to see that you survived the fire, young man. I’ve seen your handiwork in the ring. Most impressive. If you keep this up, you’ll be in my ranks before you know it.”

“That is my dream,” Golden Dragon said, still looking down. “Thank you for the kind words, Your Highness.”

“You are most welcome,” the Emperor replied. “Now, stand up. I don’t like seeing one of my most promising young men kneeling in filth.”

Golden Dragon stood and raised his head. Tonglong noticed that the boy looked slightly nervous. Strangely, the nervousness did not appear to come from the Emperor’s presence. Golden Dragon seemed to be looking right through the Emperor, in the direction of the temple.

Xie, the *Scorpion,* cleared his throat and looked at Tonglong. Tonglong met his critical gaze.

“If LaoShu is dead,” Xie said, “then our only remaining lead is the foreign boy. Do you have any news of him?”

“We expect an update momentarily,” Tonglong replied.

Xie nodded, folding his enormous arms. "Then we will wait here with you."

Tonglong grated his teeth and turned away. Fortunately, they didn't have to wait long. A moment later, Tonglong heard muffled shouts from the pit entrance tunnel. All eyes turned to the large doorway in the pit.

A breathless young guard appeared, waving his arms frantically. "He's gone! He's gone!"

"Who is gone?" Tonglong asked.

"The round eye," the guard said. "His cell door is open and the soldiers who were guarding him are dead."

"Dead?" Tonglong said. "Were you able to identify them?"

"Yes, sir," the guard replied. "The fire never made it that far. Their bodies are in perfect condition."

"How were they killed?" Tonglong asked. "The foreigner was known to carry two short *qiang*s beneath his robe—"

"Don't be ridiculous," Xie interrupted. "LaoShu's men took his *qiang*s when they arrested him. He was unarmed."

"That's right," the guard said from the pit. "I disarmed the foreign boy myself before we locked him up. Besides, they were not shot."

"How did they die, then?" Tonglong asked. "Smoke?"

"They appeared to have been crushed to death, sir," the guard said. "The strange thing is, there is no evidence of what they were crushed with."

Tonglong paused. There was only one person he

knew of who could accomplish such a feat. He looked over at his mother, and she mouthed the same name that had come to his mind—*HaMo.*

Tonglong turned to say something to the Emperor, and a glint of sunlight flickered in the distance. Tonglong glanced back at Golden Dragon and saw that he was still staring at the temple.

Tonglong squinted into the setting sun and scanned the temple's ornate roof. A pair of angry dragons scowled back at him from the roof's steep, upturned corners. Behind one of the statues, something flickered again, like wet, polished metal reflecting the day's final rays.

"Take cover, Your Highness!" Tonglong shouted. He grabbed the Emperor by the arm and began to run toward a line of nearby buildings. As he ran, Tonglong glanced back into the pit.

Golden Dragon was gone.

CHAPTER 6

Ying sat hunkered down behind an ornate stone dragon on a corner of the temple rooftop. He had a clear line of sight, three loaded *qiang*s, and a burning desire to exact revenge.

Standing in the open before him were Tonglong, AnGangseh, Xie, the Emperor, and his former brother, Long, now called Golden Dragon.

Who should fall first? Ying mused.

He raised a *qiang* to his shoulder, resting the long metal barrel on the head of the stone dragon. He'd only had limited training with these foreign weapons, and the current conditions were far from ideal. He had the sun to his back, which was a good thing, but the wind was blowing hard from left to right. *Qiang* ball accuracy was questionable enough at close distances. At this range, it was almost complete guesswork, especially with a strong crosswind. He knew the chances of hitting three or even two targets were remarkably slim.

Ying lowered his head and stared along the length of the *qiang*'s barrel, considering his options. All five targets were appealing, but there really was no question about who deserved to fall first.

Ying lined up the end of the *qiang* barrel with the center of Tonglong's chest, then carefully adjusted it up and left to account for the projectile's inevitable drift and drop. He took a deep breath, exhaled evenly, and began to squeeze the trigger.

And then Tonglong grabbed the Emperor and began to run.

Ying cursed as Tonglong, AnGangseh, the Emperor, and Xie headed for cover.

Ying knew he would never be able to hit a moving target at this distance. He let them go.

This was all Long's fault. Long had been staring at him for quite some time, and Tonglong had glanced back at Long before breaking into a run. Ying wished he knew how to mask his *chi*.

Dragons like Long possessed unusually large amounts of *chi*, or life energy, and they had an uncanny ability to sense other dragons' *chi* over great distances. Ying had always guessed that his own *chi* was strong. Now he was sure of it.

Ying turned his *qiang* toward the pit to take a shot at Long, but Long was no longer there. He was probably hiding behind one of the huge roof timbers inside the pit. Ying leaned over the edge of the rooftop to get a better angle of sight into the pit arena, and Tonglong suddenly shouted from the distance, "Straight over your heads, men!"

Two armed soldiers sprang to life below Ying from inside the temple's front door. Ying jumped to his feet and shoved the *qiang* in his hands into the tattered blanket alongside the other two weapons. The *qiang*s would be useless while he was on the move.

"There he is!" one of the soldiers shouted from below.

Click . . . fizz . . . BANG!

A *qiang* ball smashed into a clay roof tile between Ying's feet. He hoisted the *qiang*s over his shoulder and began to run due west along the steep rooftop.

Click . . . fizz . . . BANG!

A second *qiang* ball whizzed past Ying's ear. He glanced down and saw the soldiers drop their smoking *qiang*s. Rather than reload, they began to chase after him from the ground.

Ying slowed, allowing the two soldiers to catch up. As they neared, he threw his bundle of *qiang*s to the ground in front of them.

Click . . . fizz . . . BANG!

One of the *qiang*s triggered on impact, the lead ball lodging itself in the ankle of the first soldier. "Owwwww!" the man howled, and bent over, grabbing his injured leg.

Ying leaped off the rooftop with his arms spread

wide, coming down hard on the center of the wounded soldier's back.

"Ooofff," the man exclaimed as he hit the earth.

Ying stepped off the soldier, and the man twisted his head up to look at Ying. Ying planted a boot heel into the side of the soldier's head. The man went limp.

Ying turned to face the second soldier and scowled, curling his lips back over his sharpened teeth. He flicked out his forked tongue.

The soldier closed his eyes.

"Look at me!" Ying shrieked.

Quivering, the soldier opened one eye.

Ying cocked his right arm back and thrust an eagle-claw fist forward, his fingertips curled in tight against his palm. The soldier had enough sense to jump sideways and turn his head, but he was still too slow. Ying clipped the man behind the ear, and the soldier collapsed in a heap, out cold.

Ying heard Tonglong shout from the direction of the former fight club, "Surround the temple, men!"

A war cry erupted from several dozen soldiers, and Ying's carved eyebrows rose up. The men in the pit arena must have come up to ground level. He picked up the bundle of *qiang*s and began to run again. Ying reached the rear corner of the temple and rounded it at top speed.

He should have known better.

Ying felt something like a tree trunk slam into his shins, and his legs were suddenly swept out from under him. He twisted sideways as he fell and saw his former brother Long catch him by the collar.

Ying's legs and hip slammed to the ground hard enough to rattle his teeth. However, the rest of his body remained upright, held firm in Long's powerful grasp.

Ying hadn't run into a tree. Long had kicked his feet out from under him.

Ying snarled.

Long cocked his left arm back and formed a fist. He raised the oversized knuckle of his middle finger up, supported the finger with his thumb, and poised it to slam into Ying's face. A dragon fist.

"Don't make me use this," Long whispered. "Grab your bundle and follow me. Hurry, if you value your life."

Long released Ying's collar and headed toward an open doorway at the rear of the temple.

Tonglong began to shout from the front of the temple, "Spread out, men! We have him right where we want him!"

Ying heard boots coming his way. He grabbed the *qiang*s and slipped inside the doorway after Long.

CHAPTER 7

Long silently closed the door behind Ying and bolted it shut. They were in a large room, dimly lit by the setting sun peeking in through gaps where the building's outer walls met the roofline. Long signaled for Ying to follow him through the shadows.

"Why are you helping me?" Ying whispered.

Long didn't reply. He just turned and walked away.

Ying scowled. He wanted to smash Long for his quiet arrogance. However, Ying knew that he had to keep his temper in check. At least, for now. He followed patiently behind Long, carefully scanning the room.

Ying had been inside the Jinan City Temple before, but never this particular area. All around them were stacks of dusty mismatched items—a statue arm here, a broken incense urn there. When they were well clear of the door, Ying tried another question. He kept his tone as even as possible and his voice low.

"Where are we?"

This time, Long answered. "We're in the back room where the temple-keepers store their junk. There is a secret tunnel that leads here from the fight club. The temple-keepers don't even know about it."

Long headed over to a small rug and kicked it aside. He ran the fingers of one hand along a narrow floorboard and pressed down on one end. That end of the board sank downward, while the opposite end popped up.

Ying watched as Long lifted a trapdoor.

"You go first," Long whispered.

Ying looked into the narrow hole and saw a flimsy bamboo ladder. A small lantern flickered on the ground next to it.

"Hurry," Long said, his eyes now pleading.

Ying placed the bundle of *qiang*s next to the hole and climbed down. Once he reached the bottom, Long handed him the *qiang*s and came down himself, repositioning the rug above them as he closed the trapdoor.

Ying took a step back, gripping the chain whip around his waist. It seemed Long had no intention of harming him, but it was better to be safe than sorry.

Long picked up the lantern, hunched over, and headed into a low, narrow tunnel.

Ying hoisted the *qiang*s over his shoulder and followed, hunched over, until they came to a small underground room. Long placed the lantern on a makeshift shelf, and Ying saw that the entire room was filled with trinkets, much like the back room of the temple.

"LaoShu made this tunnel so that he could secretly steal items from the temple," Long said. "He sent me there many times. He and I were the only people who knew about this tunnel and storeroom. Now that he is gone, you should be safe here."

Ying looked around. The room and tunnel were simply constructed, probably dug by fight club prisoners who would have never survived their very next trip into the pit arena. No witnesses.

Ying turned to Long and wondered again why Long was doing this. He stared his former brother in the eye, and Long spoke as if reading his mind.

"I heard that you were seen leaving the burning fight club with Hok, Seh, Fu, and Malao," Long said. "You saved all four of them. I felt I should return the favor."

"Why?" Ying asked.

"Because they are my brothers and sister. It is the honorable thing to do."

Ying scoffed, "Your honor might get you killed."

"Possibly."

"What were *you* doing in the fight club?" Ying asked. "You used to hate fighting."

"I still do," Long replied. "Except Grandmaster told me and the others that we must change the Emperor's heart. I hope to win the championship and join his ranks. I will make changes from the inside out."

"You are wasting your time," Ying said. He patted the bag of *qiang*s. "This is how you make change."

"No," Long said. "Brute force never changes people. People need to change themselves."

Ying smirked. "If you say so."

Long turned away and took a small candle from the shelf. He lit it with the lantern and gave the candle to Ying.

"I held a bit of hope that you would join me in some way," Long said. "After all, you and I want the same thing—change. However, I can tell that you are neither interested nor capable of handling things my way." He pointed to a strange glass object on the shelf. It was half filled with sand and very large. "That is called an hourglass, or in this case a six-hourglass. LaoShu stole it from a foreigner. Turn it upside down and the sand will slowly pour from the top segment to the bottom. Once the sand has stopped flowing, six hours will have passed. Flip it over now, and leave when the time has elapsed. It will still be dark then and the soldiers should be resting at that time. Go back out the way we came in, and don't worry about locking the temple's exit door. By the time anyone discovers it, you will be long gone."

"You're leaving?" Ying asked.

"Yes. I've already been away for too long."

"Where are you going?"

"To join the search for you!" Long said with a wink.

“Where will you go? I will do everything I can to direct the search away from your destination.”

Ying glanced at the bundle of *qiang*s. He knew exactly where he’d be going, but he didn’t want to tell Long. “I’m not sure,” Ying lied.

“You should go to the wharf and attempt to arrange passage to some place far from Jinan,” Long said. “I will keep my team away from that area.”

“You will stay clear of the waterfront?” Ying asked. “How do I know I can trust you?”

Long stared at Ying. “Because I am a dragon.”

Ying returned the stare, but Long didn’t flinch. Ying felt *chi* radiating from Long like heat from a flame. Long was without question a dragon. A strong one.

Ying waited for Long to say more, but Long only offered a slight bow. Ying returned the courtesy.

Long picked up the lantern and walked quickly away without so much as a parting glance. If Long was offended, Ying didn’t care. Long would still keep his word. Likewise, Ying would keep his word to meet with his former brothers and sister at the wharf after sunset tomorrow. In the meantime, he saw no reason not to get some rest here in the tunnel.

Ying took a deep breath and exhaled. The earthy odor reminded him of the time he used to spend alone in Cangzhen’s escape tunnels. For some reason, he had always been happiest alone and underground.

Comfortable and relaxed, Ying flipped the hourglass, closed his eyes, and drifted off to sleep.

CHAPTER 8

Ying woke some hours later, completely refreshed. He sat up in the dim underground room and saw that the candle had burned down to a short stub and the vast majority of sand had sifted to the lower half of the hourglass. It was time to go.

Ying stood and wrapped his chain whip around his waist, noticing a pile of luxurious white silk in one corner. He tore a piece free and tied it across his face, then grabbed the *qiang*s.

Ying made it through the tunnel and temple back room without any problems. Once outside, he felt as if he had the entire city to himself. He could not see, hear, or sense another soul. The soldiers were most likely resting, as Long had suggested, and the civilians would be under curfew. Anyone who wasn't part of

Tonglong's forces would be forbidden to walk the streets until daybreak.

Ying glanced up at the clear night sky. The storm had moved on, leaving a humid late-summer stickiness in its wake. It was going to be a warm day. He could tell by the position of the moon that the sun would be rising in a couple of hours. He needed to get moving.

Ying headed for the waterfront. He wanted to scout the area where he was to meet Hok that evening. He also wanted to see someone about bartering the *qiangs*. His bruised ribs and shoulders were sore from lugging them around, and they weren't exactly the most subtle weapons to carry. What he needed was a short *qiang*.

A short *qiang* would be very difficult to come by, but Ying knew a man who specialized in finding hard-to-locate goods. Understandably, his warehouse was located in the heart of the Jinan wharf, the region's trading hub.

The man's name was HukJee, or *Black Pig* in Cantonese. He was the ringleader of a vast underground network that distributed black-market goods. If you had enough money, HukJee could get it for you, no matter what "it" was.

Ying had met HukJee after winning an impressive string of fights at the Jinan Fight Club. Ying had been an unknown fighter at the time, and HukJee had won a lot of money by betting on him. Ying had a hunch HukJee would remember him.

What Ying wanted was simple enough. He planned

to trade all three of his long *qiang*s for one short one. Ying thought the deal was fair. If HukJee's opinion differed, Ying felt confident he could persuade him otherwise.

With the blanket full of *qiang*s over his shoulder, Ying hugged the moon shadows for more than two hours, staying out of sight. Several times, he circled back upon himself to check if anyone was following him. No one was.

Ying reached HukJee's warehouse as the sun was rising. The building was situated on the crowded bank of the mighty Yellow River, surrounded on three sides by docks. Each dock contained several slips of various sizes, and each slip was filled with some sort of vessel.

In the morning glow, Ying saw small and large Chinese junks, as well as a wide range of skiffs and a few foreign boats he couldn't identify. This was a busy place.

Although the curfew must still be active, no one at the wharf seemed to pay any attention to it. Dockworkers were busy loading and unloading vessels, carrying items to and from the warehouse's many doors.

Breakfast was being prepared on several of the boats, and tantalizing aromas twisted Ying's stomach into knots. He hadn't eaten in almost two days, and his last meal had been nothing more than a few handfuls of raw vegetable trimmings he'd plucked from a trash pile.

Ying stifled his hunger pains and continued toward

HukJee's front door. As he approached, he felt someone watching him. Several people, in fact. Ying adjusted the white silk across his face, doubtful that any of them would recognize him. He glanced at his Pit Cleaner's uniform, and his heart skipped a beat. People who tended to frequent places like HukJee's also tended to frequent the fight club. He hadn't thought of that.

Ying hurried the rest of the way to HukJee's warehouse entrance and banged on the front door with his fists. It was still early, but hopefully an ambitious businessman like HukJee would already be in his office.

"Go away," a deep voice mumbled from behind the door. "Come back after breakfast."

Ying heard someone slurp loudly, then belch. Ying tried the door and found that it was unlocked. He pushed it open.

Inside, Ying saw a small front office occupied by a huge Chinese man. The man had a gigantic head, unusually dark skin, a piglike nose, and more chins than Ying could count. Creamy rice porridge dripped off the man's lower lip onto a large table covered with an unbelievable amount of food. It was HukJee, *Black Pig.* Flanking the doorway were two huge men, both covered with thick muscles from their ears to their ankles. The men scowled at Ying and folded their impressive arms.

HukJee scowled at Ying, too. He wiped drivel from his chin with a stubby forearm. "How rude," he said. "Who do you think you are? You were not invited."

Ignoring the muscle-bound men, Ying put the bundle of *qiang*s under one arm and stepped through the doorway. He closed the door behind him and ripped the silk from his face.

"Ying!" HukJee proclaimed, his round face breaking into a smile. "Why didn't you just say so? Come in, come in!" HukJee tried to stand, but his enormous belly was wedged beneath the table. He shrugged and sat back down.

Ying cringed, and HukJee laughed. "I suppose I could be stuck in worse places than the breakfast table," HukJee said. "I'd offer to have you join me, but as you can see, I barely have enough food here to feed a starving mouse, let alone two grown men like us."

Ying glanced at the mountain of food. He didn't reply.

HukJee looked at the men guarding the door. "Why don't the two of you go get some fresh air? Leave me alone to catch up with my old acquaintance."

The bodyguards nodded and left.

HukJee shoved a salted egg into his enormous maw and muttered, "You do know that there is a healthy price on your head, don't you?"

"I assumed as much," Ying replied.

"Well, you have nothing to fear from me," HukJee said, swallowing. "I learned long ago never to burn any bridges, no matter how unstable they may appear. I can't give you refuge, but I see no reason why we can't make a deal or two. I see you've brought something. Is that a bundle of *qiang*s?"

“Yes.”

“Excellent. I can never have enough of those. They’re worth their weight in gold, you know.”

“I’m not interested in gold,” Ying said. “I want a short *qiang*. Do you have any?”

“I might,” HukJee replied, leaning back in his chair. “What do you have in mind?”

Ying placed the bundle on the ground and unwrapped it. He laid two of the *qiang*s side by side and picked up the third. “I want to trade these three long *qiang*s for a short one.”

HukJee scratched one of his many chins. “Interesting. I don’t suppose any of them are loaded?”

Ying smirked and aimed the *qiang* in his arms at HukJee’s huge head. “This one is.”

“I see. Are you saying I don’t have a choice in this matter?”

“Of course you have a choice. You just might not like all your options.”

“All right, then,” HukJee said. “Anything else?”

“I need a new robe and pants,” Ying replied. “Black silk, with an extra piece to use as a mask.” He glanced at the table. “I also want some of your breakfast.”

HukJee burst into laughter. “Put the *qiang* down, Ying. Your offer is both reasonable and amusing. No one has ever threatened to kill me for my breakfast!” He clapped his fat hands once loudly, and Ying heard a flurry of footsteps outside. “My men are coming back. If they see that *qiang* in your hands, they will show you what they can do with theirs. Then you’ll miss the best breakfast of your life. That would be a shame, wouldn't it?"

Ying heard the door begin to open and he let the *qiang* slip through his fingers to his side. He kept his hand on the end of the barrel, far from the trigger.

"Wise choice," HukJee said.

One of the bodyguards stepped into the office. "Sir?"

HukJee smiled. "I need you to round up a few things. The list is short. Be quick about it; our guest is in a hurry."

A quarter of an hour later, Ying pushed himself away from HukJee's breakfast table, completely stuffed. He was certain he'd never eaten that much food before.

"Enjoy yourself?" HukJee asked.

Ying moaned and nodded. "It was delicious."

HukJee grinned. "Magnificent. I'd offer to have you join me for my midmorning snack, but I believe your goods have arrived."

Ying turned and looked out of the office door. One of the bodyguards approached, holding a brown leather bag.

"Please take a look," HukJee said. "Let me know if you are satisfied."

Ying stood from the table and the man handed him the bag. Inside was a short *qiang*, unloaded, plus lead balls, wadding, fire stones, a ramrod, and a horn of black powder. There were also black silk clothes and a wide black silk scarf that a woman might use to tie up her hair.

Ying glared at the bodyguard. "A scarf?"

The man shrugged. "The workers in back said that was all we had."

HukJee chuckled. "What about the *qiang*, Ying?"

"I like it," Ying replied, closing the leather bag. "The ammunition is a nice surprise. A pleasure doing business with you."

"Another satisfied customer," HukJee said. "Wonderful!"

Ying offered HukJee a slight bow.

HukJee bowed back as best he could with his stomach still wedged beneath the table. "Come back anytime, Ying. Just be sure to leave your attitude at the door. Treat me fairly, and I'll do the same for you."

"I'll remember that," Ying replied. He quickly tied the black scarf across his face and left.

Ying crossed the docks at a brisk pace, hurrying to find a place to change his clothes before the sun rose any higher. He zigged and zagged through four different streets before settling on a narrow alley between two tall apartment buildings. He changed quickly, shoving the Pit Cleaner's uniform and the swatch of white silk he'd had on his face beneath a small pile of rotting lumber. The new clothes were of the finest quality and fit him well. He adjusted the black silk scarf across his face, tied his chain whip around his waist, and was about to step back onto the street when he froze. He felt that someone was watching him.

Ying sank low and poked his head quickly out of the alley. At the far end of one of the buildings, he saw a man's shadow. Someone was hiding around the corner. Ying could have kicked himself. He should have been more careful leaving HukJee's.

Ying slipped the leather bag over his shoulder and quietly untied the chain whip from around his waist. He placed the chain's handle in his right hand and the weighted tip in his left. He silently wound each end of the chain around his hands until he had two metal-wrapped fists with a length of chain as long as his arm dangling between them.

Ying stepped out of the alley without making a sound and hurried toward the building's far corner. As he reached it, the shadow moved and Ying leaped high into the air, just in time. A big man with brown hair and round eyes had been expecting him. The man let out a roar and burst around the corner, swinging a large boat oar exactly where Ying's knees would have been.

The giant's mighty swing left him off balance, and Ying slammed a metal-clad fist into his jaw. The big man rocked back on his heels but must have had a chin made of iron because he shook off the blow. The man dropped the oar and dove straight at Ying.

Ying leaped into the air again, and the huge man missed him a second time. The giant landed sprawled on the ground, face-first, and Ying spun 180 degrees in the air, landing on the man's back in a sitting position. Ying wrapped his legs around the man's midsection and looped the chain whip around the man's thick neck. Ying leaned way back, cutting off the supply of air to the giant's lungs, as well as the supply of blood to his brain.

The big man thrashed wildly, clawing at the chain, but slipped into unconsciousness after just a few heartbeats.

Ying released the tension on the chain immediately. He didn't want to kill the man. He had a few questions to ask him first.

Ying unlocked his legs and was about to unwind the chain from his hands when he heard someone speak in heavily accented Mandarin Chinese.

"For a man who wears women's scarves, you fight pretty well."

Several men laughed, and Ying looked behind him. Six men stepped out of the shadows, each holding a short *qiang* in one hand and a strange sword in the other. They were all round eyes.

Ying started to unwind the chain whip from his hands, but a small man at the front of the group shook his head. "Leave your shackles on, Ying. You're coming with us."

CHAPTER 9

Ying found himself being led through a maze of back alleys and side streets, his hands bound with his own chain whip. Six heavily armed round eyes surrounded him while a seventh, the giant, led the way. The giant had just returned to consciousness and was still groggy. He weaved from side to side as he walked, Ying's leather bag swinging wildly over one of his wide shoulders.

"Where are you taking me?" Ying asked the group.

The small man who had spoken to Ying earlier smiled and said, "Sorry, we no speak Chinese."

The group laughed.

Ying bit his lip. He was fighting mad, but he knew

he was in no position to do anything. He might be able to take out one or two of the round eyes, but they all had *qiang*s and those strange swords. The swords were long and thin like a Chinese straight sword, but curved. They had a large, wide guard over the handle to protect the user's hand. Ying had seen them before, carried by round eyes in attendance at the fight clubs. The swords were called cutlasses. Ying had always wanted to test his skills against a man with one of those. Perhaps he would have his chance yet.

They eventually stopped behind an ordinary-looking single-story building. The small round eye turned to Ying and said, "Be on your best behavior. You're about to meet your new boss."

The small man stepped up to the back door and knocked two times, then three times, then once. The door opened, and Ying was shoved inside.

It took a moment for Ying's eyes to adjust to the room's dim light, but after blinking several times he had no doubt who he was looking at. Fu, Malao, and Seh sat at a large table, along with several adult round eyes. At the head of the table, the place of highest honor, sat Hok.

Hok frowned at Ying. "You weren't supposed to come down to the waterfront until this evening."

"I had some business to attend to," Ying replied.

"You made a mistake," Hok said. "That's not like you. It's a good thing Charles' friends found you before Tonglong's men did."

Ying's eyes narrowed.

"Remove his mask," Hok said to the round eyes nearest Ying. "Unwrap his chain whip, too."

"Are you sure you want him free?" the small man asked. "He seems to be quite a skilled fighter."

"He gave me his word that he will cooperate," Hok said. "Do as I ask, for Charles' sake."

"If you think he can help Charles, then okay," the small man said. He unwrapped the chain whip from Ying's hands, and Ying snatched it away.

The small man raised his *qiang* to Ying's head.

"Let him keep the chain whip," Hok said. "Return any other weapons you may have taken from him, too."

"But he carried a *qiang*," the small man protested, "and ammunition."

"His word is good," Hok said. "Return them, please."

Ying removed the silk scarf from his face himself, and one of the round eyes handed him the leather bag. Ying checked inside. Everything was as he'd left it.

"Come," Hok said to Ying. "Have a seat. We need to discuss a few things."

"I'll stand," Ying said. He wasn't about to sit in an inferior position to Hok.

"As you wish," Hok replied. "I have some new information to share. HaMo has Charles, and he wants to make an exchange."

"HaMo?" Ying said. "The former bandit?"

Hok nodded. "He contacted us here through Charles' friends. It seems HaMo snatched Charles from a holding cell while the Jinan Fight Club was burning. He wants me to meet him alone to exchange Charles for the dragon scroll map that Seh carries."

Ying glanced at Seh, then back at Hok. "You're not going to do it, are you?"

"We don't have any other choice," Hok said. "We took a vote and decided I should do it."

"You didn't let me vote," Ying said.

Hok didn't reply.

"You have no idea what you're giving up with that scroll," Ying said, frustrated. "Don't do it."

"I am going to do it," Hok said. "Unless you can think of something better."

Ying tried to calm himself. "Where are you supposed to meet him?"

"On a barge anchored in the middle of the river. Downstream, tonight. Just me."

"You're walking into a trap," Ying said.

"You don't know that."

"No?" Ying asked. "HaMo double-crossed the bandits by allowing me and Tonglong access to their secret mountain fortress. He lived as one of them for more than ten years and sold them out for gold. What makes you think he'll keep his word with you?"

Hok didn't answer.

Ying stared at her. He could tell that she was going to go, and nothing was going to stop her. "At least let me look at the scroll map before you give it away, along with your life."

"I don't know about this—" Seh began to say.

Ying turned to him. "I was promised time with the scroll as part of our deal. Show it to me."

Fu growled and looked at Hok. "But Ying isn't going to do anything," Fu said. "That means we don't have a deal anymore. Throw him out of here."

Ying ground his teeth. He needed to take a different approach. "Show me the scroll, Hok, and I'll come up with a plan. I give you my word."

Hok rubbed her temples. "I don't know—"

"I have nothing to lose and everything to gain by helping you," Ying said. "Give me a quarter of an hour with the map, and I will make sure you leave HaMo's boat alive. All of you can stand over me while I study the map, if you wish. Bind my hands and feet. I don't care. A quarter of an hour, that's all I ask in exchange for an insurance policy on your life. What do you say?"

"I say we take another vote," Malao offered. "I vote to let Ying help. So what if we show him the map? He'll probably get squashed by HaMo, anyway." He shrugged.

"No way," Fu growled. "I say we throw Ying out now."

Malao poked Seh in the arm, and Ying saw Seh's snake slither beneath his sleeve. "What do you think, Seh?" Malao asked.

Seh didn't reply.

Hok stood. "I vote that we let Ying help," she said. "It's up to you, Seh."

Seh waited a long time before answering. "We should let Ying help."

"No!" Fu roared.

"That's enough, Fu," Hok said. "It is decided."

Fu slammed his fist into the tabletop, but remained quiet. Ying was impressed. Back at Cangzhen, Fu would have continued to complain for hours over something like this.

Hok sat back down. "There is one more thing we still need to discuss. Since HaMo knows where we are, we will need to find a different place to hide. I suggest once we free Charles, the four of us travel to PawPaw's house."

"PawPaw?" Ying said. "*Grandmother?* Who is that?"

"A woman who has helped us tremendously in the past," Hok replied. "I would hate to impose on her again, but I don't know where else to go."

"PawPaw's house makes sense," Seh said.

"If it's good enough for you two, it's good enough for me," Malao added.

"That's fine with me," Fu said. "As long as Ying isn't coming."

"Then it is decided," Hok said. "Even if something should happen to me, the rest of you should go to PawPaw's, just to be safe." She looked at Ying. "Would you like to see the scroll map now?"

"The sooner, the better," Ying said. "Perhaps it will give me some inspiration for a plan."

"Please show him the scroll, Seh," Hok said.

Seh pulled the dragon scroll map from the small of his back and laid it on the table. Ying fought the urge to lunge for the scroll. He reached out, taking it carefully with both hands. Ying unrolled it and immediately felt energized. It was the same feeling he got just before a lightning storm hit. He noticed that the hair on his arms was standing on end.

As the initial excitement faded, Ying began to look the scroll over. He realized right away that it wasn't old. It was a recently made copy. He turned to Seh. "What happened to the original?"

"I modified it so that it was no longer accurate and let Tonglong steal it," Seh said. "This is an exact copy of the unmodified version. I . . . made it when I could still see."

Ying grinned. "Good trick," he said. "I bet you drove Tonglong crazy."

Seh nodded.

The small round eye peeked over Ying's shoulder. "Wait, that's not a map. It's just a sketch of a person. Those are pressure points, right?"

"I saw a sketch on the other side, too," a different round eye said. "Looked like *chi* meridians to me."

Hok pushed a lantern toward Ying. "There *are* sketches on both sides. Hold the scroll in front of the light, Ying, and watch how the two sketches blend together."

Ying followed Hok's instructions and, sure enough, a map came clearly into focus. Seh had done an amazing job. Ying had traveled quite a bit during his days in the fight clubs, and he clearly recognized that the main *chi* meridian channel running from the figure's head to its belly button was the Grand Canal, China's great north/south waterway.

The round eyes began to chatter around Ying in their native tongue, and Ying tuned them out. He set about memorizing every detail of the map. It wasn't all that difficult, as he'd long ago memorized pressure point and *chi* meridian charts. He aligned the places he'd traveled with the different sections of the map, and in no time Ying could tell what each major area represented.

The head of the figure symbolized Peking, China's capital and home of the Emperor's fabled palace fortress, the Forbidden City. The main *chi* meridian running from hand to hand represented the Yellow River. Different pressure points highlighted different cities, including Jinan. The map was a work of genius.

Ying thought about the *chi* meridians shown in the sketch and realized that they were all rivers, not roads. Most dragons were water creatures, and the mapmaker had made waterways the key to this dragon scroll map. Ying had always felt more connected to the earth than to water, but perhaps he would come to feel closer to water over time. It appeared as though he would be spending a lot of time on it, following the map to its end point far to the south.

A thought came to Ying, and he paused. *A water creature! Of course!*

Ying hastily rolled up the scroll map and handed it to Hok with a gleam in his eye. He had the beginnings of a plan.

"Okay, little sister," Ying said. "Here is what we are going to do. . . ."

CHAPTER 10

Tonglong sat at the stern of his dragon boat with twenty of his best men. They were well hidden by heavy brush and the approaching darkness. Beyond them, anchored downstream in the center of the Yellow River, was HaMo's rented barge.

Tonglong adjusted his long ponytail braid and glanced down at the note he'd received from HaMo earlier in the day. He crumpled it and threw it overboard.

The note had begun oddly enough with an apology. HaMo had said that he was sorry for having crushed two of Tonglong's men to death. He also apologized for taking Charles. However, he said that he was certain Tonglong would quickly get over these things after hearing his proposal.

HaMo said that he was going to use Charles as bait to capture Hok, along with the fabled dragon scroll map that he knew Tonglong wanted. HaMo had managed to squeeze information out of Charles and learned that the dragon scroll map in Tonglong's possession had been altered. However, Hok's brother Seh had a copy of the correct map. HaMo said that he would soon have it and offered to exchange Charles, Hok, and the map for ten thousand gold pieces.

HaMo had designated a place to meet Tonglong the next morning to make the exchange. However, Tonglong was not about to give ten thousand gold pieces to anyone. He would take what he wanted. A few hours ago, his men had discovered the location of HaMo's rendezvous with Hok, and they had disposed of a backup team HaMo had positioned in this very location. Tonglong's men were learning fast, and he was proud of them. HaMo was in for a big surprise.

"Sir," a soldier whispered from the bow of the dragon boat. "A skiff is approaching."

Tonglong squinted in the fading light and saw a well-cared-for skiff heading downstream toward HaMo's boat. Standing at the back of the skiff, steering along with the current, was a girl with short hair in a battered white dress. It was Hok, and she was alone.

Tonglong watched as Hok neared HaMo's ancient wooden barge. The barge was perhaps thirty paces long and ten paces wide, and the rear section contained what appeared to be a small house complete with a roof. Light spilled out from several windows.

The barge floated low in the water and was anchored at its bow. It pointed nose-first, upstream. Hok pulled alongside the barge on Tonglong's side of the river. Tonglong could see everything.

A man hurried out of the barge's small house and leaned over the vessel's low side rail, facing Hok. He helped her tie the skiff off, then hauled her aboard. The man pushed Hok roughly into the little house, and Tonglong heard a door slam closed.

Tonglong signaled to his men. They would give HaMo a quarter of an hour to subdue Hok, and then they would make their move.

CHAPTER 11

Ying hung on to the slippery rope with all his might, nothing but a hollow reed connecting him to the surface. He rode the river's current as best he could, wondering how Cheen and Sum, the eel twins he'd heard about at the bandit stronghold, ever managed to do this on a regular basis.

Hok's skiff stopped suddenly with a loud *thump*, and Ying knew that they had finally reached HaMo's barge. He held fast to the rope and waited, the current tugging at him, urging him downstream.

Above the surface, Ying could make out random banging noises. The skiff was being tied off to the barge. He saw the skiff rock slightly, then float noticeably higher in the water. Hok had boarded HaMo's vessel.

Ying counted to one hundred, then took a deep breath. He spat out the reed, dove beneath the barge, and swam across the current, surfacing on the other side of the large vessel. He reached up, grabbed hold of the barge's low railing, and silently pulled his shoulders and chest out of the water.

Ying looked across the deck. It was almost dark now, but he could see well enough to know that there was no one on it. Lights burned inside some sort of living quarters that looked just like a small house. Hok must be inside there.

Ying pulled himself the rest of the way out of the water onto the barge. He stifled a groan as his healing ribs strained. Once aboard, he lay down and untied his chain whip from his waist, folding it into his right fist. He wished he could have brought his new *qiang* with him, but it would have been rendered useless after being underwater.

Ying slid on his belly over to the living quarters. He flattened himself against the outer wall on the opposite side of the house from the skiff and listened. Inside, he heard talking.

Ying rose up cautiously and peeked inside a window. The round eye Charles was sitting inside a low bamboo cage at the back of a small room. Hok was sitting on the floor next to Charles with the scroll map in her hands. HaMo stood across the cluttered room, arguing with two Chinese men whose backs were to the front door.

There wasn't much room to maneuver in there, especially with HaMo, the *Toad,* as part of the equation.

He weighed as much as three normal men and was nearly as big around as HukJee. At least, Ying's eagle-style training would prove useful here. It was famous for its close-quarters effectiveness.

Ying sank back down and thought, *HaMo plus two others against me and Hok. Not bad odds.*

Ying eased his way around to the closed front door and stood. With thoughts of his best friend, Luk, running through his head, Ying kicked the door down with a mighty back-kick. Using the momentum he already had going in that direction, he spun around and leaped through the doorway with his arms spread wide. HaMo's eyes widened, and the two henchmen turned to face Ying.

Ying landed and unfurled his chain whip forward with a powerful punching motion. The sharp weighted end buried itself deep within the first henchman's sternum, and the man dropped like a stone.

Ying yanked his chain whip free and HaMo leaned forward, grabbing the second henchman. He pulled the man in front of himself like a human shield.

Ying tried to swing his chain whip, but there just wasn't enough room. He shrieked in frustration and saw the second henchman break loose from HaMo's grip. The man lunged toward a long counter and grabbed something, then spun around and pointed it at Ying.

It was a short *qiang*.

The ear-splitting shrill of an angry bird filled the room, and Ying saw a flash of white as Hok flew past him. She knocked the *qiang* from the second henchman's hand with a lightning-quick snap-kick, and attacked the man with a flurry of elbows and crane-beak fists to the head.

The *qiang* rattled to the floor and Ying made a move for it. However, HaMo unleashed a tremendous *CROAK!* that shook the entire boat, and he hopped on top of the *qiang* before Ying could pick it up.

Ying took a step back and was surprised to see HaMo glance out of a window as if he were looking for help. Perhaps he had a backup team somewhere and that tremendous *croak* was a signal.

Ying glanced over at Hok and saw that she was now standing over the second henchman. The man was out cold.

HaMo aimed the short *qiang* at Hok. "Very impressive, little lady. Now give me the map."

Hok shook her head, and Ying noticed the map poking out of the collar of her tattered dress.

Ying took a tiny step toward HaMo. HaMo glared at him. "Make a move against me, Ying, and your little sister dies."

Ying paused. "Go ahead," he said. "I'd rather you use your only shot on her. It would save me the trouble of having to do it myself."

"You can't fool me," HaMo said. "I know you came here with her."

"Did I?" Ying asked. He began to creep forward.

"I'm warning you—" HaMo began to say, and Ying saw something flash across his field of vision. HaMo yelped, and Ying was shocked to see a small throwing knife stuck in the side of HaMo's enormous neck.

Ying glanced back at the bamboo cage and saw that Charles had removed the heel of one of his boots. The knife must have been hidden inside it.

Ying looked back at HaMo and could hardly believe his eyes. HaMo shook his huge head, and the knife popped out of his bulbous flesh as though it were some sort of child's toy. The wound was bleeding, but it didn't appear to be very deep. HaMo's mounds of fat had protected him from the throwing knife's short blade.

"What the—" Charles said.

HaMo laughed. "Better luck next time, Round Eye." He turned back to Hok. "Give me the—"

But Hok was already flying toward him. She grabbed HaMo's short *qiang* with both hands and drove her face into the back of his lumpy hand, biting him hard enough to draw blood.

"Arrr!" HaMo growled through clenched teeth. Still, he didn't let go of the *qiang*. Hok released her teeth but held firm with her hands. HaMo raised his other lumpy hand high to strike at Hok with an open palm, and Ying leaped for HaMo's raised hand, catching HaMo by the thumb.

Ying wrapped both his hands around HaMo's stubby, fat thumb and pulled back with all his might. *Control the thumb and you control the entire body* was one of his former teacher's favorite sayings.

HaMo squealed like a child and released the *qiang*, swinging his bloodied hand wildly in Ying's direction.

Out of the corner of his eye, Ying saw Hok run over to Charles with the *qiang*.

Ying kept constant pressure on HaMo's thumb, weaving back and forth to keep HaMo off balance. Ying was so busy weaving around and watching HaMo's free hand that he failed to keep an eye on HaMo's feet.

"Look out!" Charles shouted, but it was too late. Ying felt his legs sweep out from under him. Even so, Ying refused to let go of HaMo's thumb. As Ying crashed to the floor, he heard a *crack* like the sound of dry firewood in a roaring blaze. HaMo roared as the main bone in his thumb snapped in half.

Ying lost his grip on the dangling thumb half, and HaMo pulled his hand free. Ying saw HaMo bend his knees in preparation for a crushing jump, and Ying tried to roll out of the way. After half a turn, however, Ying came to a dead stop against the unconscious body of one of HaMo's henchmen.

Ying looked up in time to see HaMo leap into the air, then jolt suddenly to one side as the all-too-familiar sounds of *click . . . fizz . . . BANG!* filled the room.

The *qiang* ball hit HaMo in the left eye. His lifeless body crashed down, missing Ying by a hairsbreadth.

Ying sat up and took a deep breath. He wiped his carved brow and looked over at Charles. The round eye still held the smoking *qiang* in his hands.

Ying stood and bowed to Charles, low and deep. "Thank you. You saved my life."

Kneeling, Charles bowed back from inside the

cage. "And you've saved mine with this rescue." He smiled a ghostly white smile. "Any chance you could find a way to get me out of here?"

Ying glanced at HaMo and saw a small ring of keys tied to his enormous sash. Ying used the sharp tip of his chain whip to cut the keys free and hurried over to Charles' cage. The lock opened with the third key Ying tried.

Charles crawled out of the cage and stood on wobbly legs. He took the key ring from Ying and hobbled quickly over to a row of drawers beneath the long counter. Charles fumbled through keys until one fit, then opened a drawer and pulled out three large pouches, each bigger than a man's fist. Charles tossed one pouch to Hok and another to Ying. He kept the third pouch for himself.

Ying heard a distinct series of metallic *clink*s when he caught his pouch. Coins. He grinned.

Charles nodded. "There is something even more valuable in *here,*" he said, reaching into a different drawer. "Look."

Charles pulled out a pair of matching short *qiang*s.

"Those are yours, aren't they?" Hok asked.

Charles smiled. "Yes. I saw HaMo put them in here. I watched him all day while I pretended to sleep. This boat holds more than a few surprises. Take a look at this."

Charles walked over to a window and grabbed a large cloth resting beneath it. He yanked the cloth aside, unveiling a cannon that would take loads as large as a man's head.

Ying nodded, impressed.

"There's more, too," Charles said.

Hok shook her head. "We don't have time for this. I think HaMo might have signaled someone for help."

"That's right," Ying said. "I noticed that, too. We should leave."

Charles reached into a drawer and pulled out a spyglass. He looked through it, out the window, and Ying saw his body go rigid.

"Men, prepare your *qiang*s!" someone shouted in the distance.

Charles continued to stare. "Who is that?"

Ying scowled. He didn't have to look outside to identify the person rushing toward them in the darkness. He would recognize that cold, metallic voice anywhere.

CHAPTER 12

"Tonglong!" Ying spat. "What is he doing here?"

"Who knows," Hok replied. She grabbed a small lantern and hurried outside.

Ying rushed out onto the deck behind Hok and saw Tonglong approaching in a dragon boat with twenty soldiers. The men were paddling furiously.

"You two go on," Charles said, hurrying out of the living quarters into the darkness. "I'll stay here and distract them." He shoved his *qiang*s and the spyglass into his sash and ran over to Hok's skiff. He began untying the ropes that connected it to the barge.

"Can't we just cut the anchor rope and take this barge downstream?" Ying asked.

“It’s too slow,” Charles said. “We would only be able to travel as fast as the current. Besides, it is better if we split up. You and Hok take the skiff. I’ll see what I can do from here.”

“Let us help you—” Hok began to say.

“FIRE!” Tonglong commanded, and four *qiang*s rang out.

Ying and Hok hit the deck, flattening themselves against the damp wooden floorboards. Charles remained standing, untying the last of the skiff’s lines as *qiang* balls whistled past his head.

“Please, go!” Charles pleaded.

Hok looked at Ying, and Ying nodded. The two of them scrambled for the skiff.

“Charles, if you happen to see my brothers, please remind them to go to PawPaw’s house,” Hok said. “They will know what I am talking about.” She climbed over the barge’s low railing and into the skiff. The small lantern she carried provided just enough light to show the way.

“Aye, aye,” Charles said. “I hope to see you both soon.” He gave Hok and Ying a quick nod, then hurried back into the living quarters.

Ying leaped over the railing, landing softly in the lantern’s tiny pool of light, and they shoved off. Hok stood at the stern and began to row vigorously with the skiff’s single large oar.

“Do you want me to do that?” Ying asked.

“No,” Hok said. “You watch for trouble ahead and behind.”

"FIRE!" Tonglong commanded again, and four more shots rang out. Ying realized that the soldiers were firing in rotation. Two *qiang* balls burrowed into the side of HaMo's barge. Two more splashed into the river next to the skiff. Tonglong was getting close.

Ying looked over at the barge and saw Charles through one of the living quarters' illuminated windows. He was preparing the cannon. Tonglong must have seen Charles, too.

"New target, men!" Tonglong ordered. "Aim for the round eye on the barge! FIRE!"

Four shots cut through the night air, and Ying saw Charles duck. A moment later, Charles stood again, cool as a winter breeze. He continued preparing the cannon.

Ying looked back at Tonglong and saw the dragon boat barreling forward at terrific speed. It rammed into the side of the ancient wooden barge, and the dragon's ornate ironclad head crashed deep into the hull. The barge lilted heavily to one side as water began to rush into the gaping hole.

"Push away, men!" Tonglong ordered. "Take aim at the round eye again!"

"No!" Hok shouted. She turned to Ying. "We have to do something! They won't miss from that distance."

"I have an idea," Ying said. "Give me the dragon scroll map."

Hok hesitated, then reached into her dress and pulled out the map.

Ying snatched it away and held it high over his head with one hand, lifting the lantern with his other hand.

"Hey, Horse Hair!" Ying shouted to Tonglong. "Yeah, you, Ponytail! Is this what you want?" Ying pinched one corner of the scroll between his fingertips and let the scroll fall open. It flapped in the breeze beside the lantern.

Tonglong scoffed loudly and shouted back, "Don't worry, Dragon Boy, I'll catch up with you soon enough!"

Ying frowned. His plan to distract Tonglong wasn't working. He needed to do something more.

"Hey, Tonglong!" Ying shouted. "Watch this!"

Ying smashed the side of the lantern with the back of his hand and dangled the end of the scroll into the flames. The scroll ignited, illuminating his carved face with a flickering orange glow.

Tonglong roared, "New orders, men! Take out Ying! Whoever puts a hole in his head becomes my new number one soldier!"

*Qiang*s erupted in the night, and Ying was thrown backward as a ball of lead buried itself in his shoulder. The lantern splashed into the river and the scroll drifted into the air, consumed by fire. The map disintegrated into a hundred thousand bits of black ash that rained down around Ying's head.

At the same time, an enormous *BOOM!* rang out from the barge, followed by the thunderous crash of splintering wood and screaming men. Ying rolled over on the floor of the skiff to see Tonglong's dragon boat sinking fast. Charles had hit it at point-blank range with the cannon.

Ying scanned the tilting barge and saw an injured soldier pull himself out of the water. The man scrambled across the shifting deck into the living quarters.

A single shot rang out, and Charles emerged from the small house with a smoking *qiang* in his hands. The barge tilted further to one side, and Charles shoved the *qiang* into his sash. He scrambled onto the roof of the house and looked downstream at Ying and Hok. He waved, signaling that all was well, then dove over the side.

Ying raised his arm to acknowledge Charles' signal, but the world suddenly swooned around him. He closed his eyes for a few moments, and when he opened them again, he saw Hok leaning over him. Her lips were moving, but he couldn't hear a word.

Ying glanced at his left shoulder and was surprised to see that Hok was digging her fingers into it. She pulled out a *qiang* ball and tossed it overboard. There was blood everywhere. He didn't feel a thing.

The skiff and everything around Ying began to spin as though they were being sucked into a gigantic whirlpool. He felt light-headed, and he realized that his limbs were shaking. He was suddenly very cold.

Ying nodded weakly to Hok and saw her eyes widen. Her lips screamed—*Stay awake, Ying!*—but he heard nothing. He was so very tired.

Ying closed his eyes and slipped into unconsciousness.

CHAPTER 13

Charles pulled himself through the mighty Yellow River with smooth, powerful strokes. The *qiang*s in his sash and his heavy boots slowed him down, but he was still far ahead of Tonglong and the wounded soldiers bobbing among the wreckage of their dragon boat.

Charles estimated he would reach the shore at least a quarter of an hour ahead of any survivors. Plenty of time to make it to the safe house and update the others. He would honor Hok's request and remind Fu, Malao, and Seh to go to PawPaw's house. However, there was no way they were going without him. He had saved Hok's life once before, and he would gladly risk his own life again and again for her.

Charles would take the lead in her rescue. Malao

was only eleven years old, and Fu and Seh were just twelve and thirteen. They weren't old enough.

Charles was fifteen. He was strong and he was clever, and most importantly, he had a boat. The fastest boat in all China. It was small, but it could accommodate the four of them, plus limited supplies. And if any of the others complained about him being in charge, the overall weight would quickly be reduced. The mutineers would be left in whatever port happened to be next.

Charles knew how to keep a crew of seasoned sailors in line. He could certainly handle three children.

CHAPTER 14

"Wake up, Ying," a soft voice urged. "Breathe through your nose."

Ying opened his eyes to find he was on his back inside the skiff with Hok hovering over his head. It was daylight, and she was holding a small twig beneath his nostrils. The fresh twig had been twisted upon itself many times, and a pungent liquid was oozing forth. It smelled so acrid, Ying's eyes watered. He coughed.

"Sorry," Hok said, casting the twig aside. "*Xiang mu* tree branch. Smelling the evergreen's sap can bring unconscious people like you back to the waking world."

Ying groaned. He glanced up to see where they were and was temporarily blinded by the sun high overhead. He squinted and moaned, "What time is it?"

"Nearly midday. You've been unconscious since last night. I was beginning to question whether you were ever going to come out of it. I was lucky to have found the *xiang mu* tree nearby. I found a few other things, too." She nodded toward Ying's left shoulder. "How does it feel?"

Ying turned his head to see strips of Hok's white silk dress wrapped neatly around his upper arm and chest. The whole area felt as if it had been trampled by an ox.

"It's fine," Ying said.

"It's not fine," Hok replied. "I'm sure it hurts quite a bit. I removed a *qiang* ball from your shoulder last night, and packed the wound with horsetail plant once we arrived here." She pointed to a cluster growing nearby, close to the water's edge.

Ying looked over the side of the skiff and realized Hok had run it aground to take care of him. He nodded his thanks.

Hok nodded back.

"Where are we?" Ying whispered.

"I don't know," Hok said. "Soon after you blacked out, I went to work on your arm, quelling the bleeding as much as possible with strips of silk. Then I grabbed the oar and rowed upstream until—"

"Upstream?" Ying interrupted.

"Yes," Hok said. "I am anticipating that Tonglong will have men search for us downstream since that is the direction of the current."

"Clever," Ying said.

Hok nodded. "We shall see."

"Then what happened?"

"I continued to row upstream until the sun rose high enough that I could see the shore clearly. As soon as I found this patch of horsetail plant, I landed the boat and packed your wounds with it. After that, I went in search of the *xiang mu,* and here we are."

Ying paused and gathered his thoughts. "Why are you helping me? We were even."

"What a ridiculous question," Hok said. "People should always help one another. That's just the right thing to do."

"But I—"

"I know what you've done," Hok said. "And I can guess what you're planning to do. It doesn't matter. I am not an animal. I have compassion."

Ying groaned. He didn't know what to say. He tried to sit up but collapsed back onto the floor of the skiff.

"You've lost a lot of blood," Hok said. "You're weak. Lie still and relax. I want to go search for some *dang gui*—angelica plant—to make a blood tonic for you to drink."

Ying shook his head slowly. "No. Tonglong will be looking for us. We need to hide."

"We will deal with Tonglong when he confronts us. The problem right now is your well-being. You need medicine, so I need to find you herbs."

"Just leave me here," Ying said. "Save yourself."

Hok rolled her eyes. "Save the drama. You sound like Fu. I will help you until you can help yourself.

Besides, I have nowhere to go. I don't want to put the others in any more danger than they are already in. Charles will remind Fu, Malao, and Seh to go to Paw-Paw's house, but I've decided to stay clear of there for the time being."

Ying thought for a moment. "If you insist on helping me, I will need dragon bone."

Hok shook her head. "I will find you some real herbs. Powdered dragon bone has no medicinal value. Street vendors hawk it for ridiculous prices to take advantage of sick people."

"How would you know?" Ying challenged weakly.

"The teachers back at Cangzhen told me, including Grandmaster."

"Grandmaster did not want you to learn the truth," Ying said. "He wanted to keep the dragon-bone secrets to himself."

"Do you know what dragon bone is?" Hok asked. "It's a rock. Dragons no longer exist. They walked the earth so long ago, their remains have turned to stone. You might as well consume powdered boulders."

"You are wrong," Ying said. "The dragon's essence is still alive in it. I've felt it."

"It is all in your mind, Ying, and you are wasting vital energy arguing with me. Get some rest."

"Find some dragon bone and you will see for yourself," Ying urged. "I . . . dare you."

"Stop with the challenges," Hok said. "They are childish."

Ying scowled weakly.

Hok glanced at the pouch of coins tied to Ying's sash. "I'll tell you what. Earlier this morning, I heard signs of civilization upstream. After I make some real medicine for you, we will head that way and I will attempt to purchase some dragon bone. Hopefully, no one will be on the lookout for us. Will that make you happy?"

Ying nodded slowly. "Yes. You will see."

"We will both see," Hok said. "Now go back to sleep. I have things to do."

Ying woke beneath a large willow tree. The sun had set, and it was nearly pitch-dark around him. It took him a moment to realize that he was in the skiff and that it had been beached in a different location. He heard water lapping gently against the boat's wooden sides. Hok sat in the bow, humming softly.

"We've moved," Ying muttered.

Hok stopped humming. "Yes. I couldn't find any *dang gui,* so I shoved off and we headed upstream to the village outskirts while you slept. I have something for you."

Hok leaned toward Ying and held out a small terracotta crucible. She lifted the tiny lid, and Ying saw a fine powder inside. Dragon bone.

"This was all I could find," Hok said. "I had to get it from a black-market vendor. All the legitimate vendors said they no longer carry it because the Emperor has placed too high a tax on it. I imagine this is only enough for a few weeks if you consume it daily, but it cost more than half your coins."

“It is worth it,” Ying whispered. “You will see. Now I need you to find me a snake.”

Hok shook her head. “I know you want to mix the dragon bone with fresh snake blood. I won’t do it.”

“You . . . have to,” Ying said.

“I don’t have to do anything. I didn’t even have to get this. In fact, I probably shouldn’t have. It took me so long to find, I ran out of time to get you proper herbs.”

“Dragon bone is all I need,” Ying whispered. “It is a rejuvenator. It helps the body repair itself at a rapid rate. They say it even helps the old stay young.”

“People say lots of things,” Hok said. “This dragon bone will do nothing for you. And when it doesn’t, I don’t want to hear you complain that it didn’t work because I didn’t mix it with snake blood.”

“I won’t,” Ying said. “Just mix it with water. It won’t be as effective, but the results will be noticeable, even to you.”

Hok sighed and shook her head again. “What ratio should I use?”

“The crucible lid doubles as a measuring device. Mix one scoop of the powder with one scoop of water.”

Ying watched as Hok scanned the ground around them. She leaned out of the skiff and picked up a small section of dried tree bark that contained a curved hollow, and rinsed it in the river. Then she poured one scoop of powdered dragon bone and one scoop of water into the hollow and swirled it around. Hok held the bark to Ying’s mouth, and he drank greedily.

Ying smacked his lips. "Ahhhhhhh. You have no idea how good that makes me feel."

"If you say so," Hok said. "We should be moving on."

"Tonight?" Ying asked.

"We have no choice. If you are afraid of the dark, go back to sleep."

Ying frowned weakly. "Very funny. I thought you might be tired, that's all. It just so happens dragon bone works best while you're sleeping. Perhaps I *will* go back to sleep."

"You do that, Ying," Hok said. "Good night."

Ying woke a few hours later, but he felt as if he'd slept for days. He sat up in the skiff and winced at the pain in his shoulder. He was sore, but he no longer felt dizzy.

Ying looked over at Hok. She was at the stern, rowing them steadily upstream in the moonlight, pushing the skiff's oar from side to side with a strong, steady rhythm.

Hok blinked. "I can't believe what I'm seeing."

"What?" Ying asked. He quickly scanned the shoreline.

"You," Hok said. "You shouldn't be able to sit up like that already."

"Oh," Ying said, looking back at her. "I told you, it's the dragon bone."

Hok nodded. "It might be. Have you ever heard any other stories about dragon-bone cures?"

“Such as?”

“I don’t know, anything.”

Ying thought for a moment. “They say it has done some strange things in certain cases, like helped the deaf to hear again. They also say it has brought sight back to people blinded in certain kinds of accidents. You’re thinking about Seh, aren’t you?”

“Perhaps.”

“Well, this dragon bone is mine.”

“Of course, but perhaps I will look for more.”

“Where?” Ying asked.

“Along the river, I suppose.”

“You don’t know your way around.”

“I’ll figure it out.”

Ying thought about the map he’d memorized. The same map that he’d burned. It led far south down the Grand Canal. Perhaps he could convince Hok to travel that route while she looked for more dragon bone. He could get more dragon bone for himself, too.

“Why don’t I join you?” Ying proposed. “I’ve traveled throughout this region while participating in the fight clubs. In fact, just a bit upstream from here is the Grand Canal. We could follow that south, traveling with the canal’s current. There are a thousand villages of all sizes along the canal. We are sure to find some dragon bone there, and I doubt Tonglong will ever suspect we’ve gone that way.”

“I don’t know—”

“I need you,” Ying said, half speaking the truth. “We need each other. I can’t show my face anywhere. A scarf doesn't seem to help much. You can take care of things I might need and help me heal, and I will navigate and keep an eye on the skiff while you're out shopping for dragon bone. We can work as a team. I will make it worth your while."

"I don't want anything from you," Hok said. Then she sighed. "But I do want to help Seh. All right, I will allow you to join me as long as you make yourself useful. You can start by watching the shore for anything that looks suspicious."

Ying nodded. "You won't be sorry."

Hok didn't reply. She just continued rowing the skiff in the darkness.

Ying stifled a grin and began to scan the shoreline. He was now on the road to riches, and Hok was chauffeuring him there. He'd have to find a way to get rid of her before they got too close to the treasure, of course, but he was confident that he would think of something. There had to be a hundred different ways a powerful dragon like himself could clip the wings of a crane, if necessary.

CHAPTER 15

Tonglong unsheathed his straight sword and stormed into HukJee's office two days later. A pair of bodyguards stood on either side of the doorway, but they didn't attack. They took one look at Tonglong's extraordinarily long ponytail and shimmering sword, and they dropped to their knees, kowtowing.

Tonglong sent them away with a wave of his hand and turned to HukJee. "Where is he?"

HukJee pushed his enormous self away from the dinner table and smiled, his mouth full of food. "Where is who?" he mumbled. "And warm greetings to you, too, by the way. You'll have to teach me that trick with the sword. Those bodyguards never kowtow like that to me."

Tonglong frowned. "Now is not the time for jokes. I am looking for Ying, the kid with the carved face. I understand he was here recently."

"Ah, yes," HukJee said, interlocking his fat fingers. "The teenager with the eagle's name and the dragon's appearance. Interesting young man, that one. He offered me three long *qiang*s for a short one, plus some clothes and a bit of my breakfast. Quite a character."

"Those aren't the sort of details I'm looking for," Tonglong said. "Tell me where I can find him."

HukJee shrugged. A mountain of flesh rippled across his upper back. "I don't know. I never ask these things. It's bad for business."

"I'm making it your business," Tonglong said. "Give me your best guess."

"I really have no idea."

Tonglong took a step toward HukJee, considering whether he should slice him into bacon or short ribs, when Tonglong's mother drifted into the room through the open front door.

"There is no sssign of them on the docks," AnGangseh hissed to Tonglong from behind her black hood. "I do not think they are here."

"Of course they aren't here, AnGangseh," HukJee said. "You will only find my employees. Shame on you for not sending word that you and your son were stopping by for a chat. I would have tidied up a bit." He burped.

AnGangseh looked at Tonglong. "Did you get any information out of this disgusting excuse for a human being?"

“No,” Tonglong replied.

A smile slid up the side of AnGangseh’s face. “Let me try.” She turned to HukJee. “Do you remember the first time we met at the Jinan Fight Club?”

“How could I ever forget,” HukJee said, taking a gigantic bite out of a lamb shank. “You were a vision of loveliness.”

“You were with your nephew, correct?” AnGangseh asked.

“Yes,” HukJee mumbled. “Why do you mention him?”

“Because I thought I sssaw him outside a moment ago. I would like him to deliver a message for me.”

AnGangseh removed her hood and walked over to an open window. She poked her head outside.

Tonglong watched as his mother waved a hulking dockworker over, inviting him inside the office with a wink. The man hurried so quickly, he tripped twice over his own gigantic feet before stumbling through the door.

AnGangseh closed the door behind the big man and asked, “Do you remember me?”

“Do I ever!” HukJee’s nephew replied.

AnGangseh offered him a smile. “Lovely. Won’t you please do me the favor of closing the window shutters?”

HukJee’s nephew promptly obeyed.

“I don’t like the looks of this,” HukJee said to his nephew. “Perhaps you should leave.”

“Or perhaps you should come ssstand a little closer to me, Big Boy,” AnGangseh said in a soft voice. She beckoned to HukJee's nephew with a wiggling forefinger, and he ambled toward her like an eager puppy.

Tonglong kept his eyes on his mother's finger. As HukJee's nephew lumbered close, AnGangseh drove the long nail at the end of her wiggling forefinger into the side of the big man's neck.

HukJee's nephew dropped to the floor in convulsions, his neck instantly swelling several times its normal size.

HukJee gasped.

Within moments, HukJee's nephew stopped convulsing, his oxygen-depleted brain no longer sending signals to his oversized muscles, or anywhere else.

AnGangseh glared at HukJee. "Has your nephew delivered my message?"

HukJee wiped a tear from his eye. "Yes," he said through clenched teeth.

"And what is that message?" AnGangseh asked.

Gigantic beads of sweat began to run down HukJee's bloated forehead and cheeks. "The message is, if I don't give you any information I have, you will kill my family. Then afterward, most certainly, you will kill me. Considering how close you both are to the Emperor, I should keep in mind that there is nothing I nor anyone else can do about it."

Tonglong nodded approvingly. "I've always heard that pigs are intelligent creatures. Now I know this to be true. I will ask you one more time, HukJee—what is your best guess as to Ying's current location?"

HukJee took a deep breath and exhaled. He wiped

more tears from his eyes. "If I had to wager my life, which it appears I do, I would guess that Ying is on a quest for dragon bone."

"Dragon bone?" Tonglong said. "Why?"

HukJee shook his behemoth head. "How am I supposed to know these things? I only heard that a young girl with short hair purchased a small quantity of dragon bone in a village upstream early yesterday. Apparently, she wanted more, but everyone was sold out. She was seen leaving with another individual in a skiff. They headed farther upstream. Since rumors claim she looked just like the girl in your new wanted posters, perhaps the person with her was Ying."

"That has to be them," AnGangseh said. "She went upstream, you sssay? Clever girl."

"Indeed," Tonglong said. He glared at HukJee. "Is this all you know?"

"Yes," HukJee replied. "I swear on my life, and on the life of my poor nephew." He sniffled.

Tonglong turned away from HukJee and whispered into his mother's ear, "Where do you think they are going? Back to Kaifeng to search for the bandits?"

AnGangseh shook her head. "The Grand Canal is upstream."

"Of course," Tonglong whispered. "The map! Ying is going to follow it while looking for dragon bone. He would not have destroyed the scroll the other night unless he had another copy. The girl must be going along to help him. He knows he cannot show his face. We need to track them."

AnGangseh nodded.

Tonglong straightened and turned to HukJee. "Here are your orders, you oversized, sniveling ham hock. Send word through your network of black-market suppliers that Ying and a young girl with pale skin and short brown hair will be traveling south along the Grand Canal seeking powdered dragon bone. No one is to sell them any until further notice. Violators will have to deal with me personally. I need you to set up a system to track their positions and keep me apprised. My mother and I will be traveling that way with the Emperor in the coming weeks. We shouldn't be difficult to find. I look forward to hearing from members of your network along the way."

HukJee swallowed hard, his numerous chins jiggling. "I understand."

"Pleasure doing business with you, *Pig*," Tonglong said. He stepped over HukJee's nephew and walked out of the office, his mother slithering along beside him.

CHAPTER 16

Ying sat alone in the skiff on the bank of the Grand Canal, half a *li* south of a nameless village. He was waiting for Hok to return on foot in the fading daylight. She had visited ten similar villages over the past week and had searched each for dragon bone, but had returned empty-handed every time. Ying was beginning to lose patience.

Ying and Hok had reached the Grand Canal the first night they shoved off together, and since then the scenery had changed little. The canal was wide, more than one hundred paces across, with stone walls protecting the shores of the villages. Outside of the populated areas, however, the canal walls fell quickly away to become muddy, unprotected banks, giving the appearance of a typical river.

Ying knew that the canal stretched for more than a thousand *li* from end to end and was dug entirely by hand. It was the country's main north/south route for transporting goods and was considered one of mankind's greatest accomplishments. Some said even greater than the Great Wall.

Ying was not impressed by many things, but the thought of hundreds of thousands of men working together, digging for years to complete the Grand Canal, gave him pause. He was certain they would have been under pressure to complete it in a certain time frame, and wondered how long it actually took.

Time was something Ying felt he was running out of. While they had not encountered any major obstacles, he and Hok were not making great progress. Not only were they stopping often for Hok to fruitlessly shop for dragon bone, but there were stretches of the canal where the land sloped so steeply that locks were required to raise and lower boats.

The locks were another marvel of engineering, but one that Ying could do without. They cost money and time to navigate, and every one meant a chance that he and Hok might be recognized. Whenever possible, they would navigate the locks in the middle of the day, when boat traffic was heaviest. With so many boats jostling for position, bumping and crashing into one another, no one bothered to scrutinize Ying's masked face or Hok's turbaned head.

Outside of the locks, Ying and Hok traveled mostly at night, sharing the duties of rowing with the skiff's oar. One would row while the other slept.

During the day, they would try to find an uninhabited bank near a village where Hok could shop. While she hadn't found any dragon bone, she'd found plenty of other things to purchase. Beyond necessities such as food, Hok had replaced the herb bag that she'd lost in the fight club fire and was slowly filling it, village by village. She complained about the poor selection and inferior quality of most of the herbs, though. She especially complained about the high taxes.

Hok told Ying that the Emperor had placed a heavy tax on all medicinal herbs, so people had begun to purchase their herbs from black-market dealers, who sold items without tax. Legitimate herb vendors—who also happened to be trained doctors—were stocking fewer and fewer items, and what they had on their shelves tended to be old. Hok disliked the black-market vendors because most of them didn't have the slightest clue how the different herbs should be used, but she quickly found she had no choice but to buy from them.

Hok told Ying that if they could remain in any given village for two or three days, the vendors promised they could get her most any item she desired, including dragon bone. The black-market vendors in every village were part of the same vast network that had runners carrying items between the villages and larger cities daily. Ying and Hok discussed this and decided that waiting that long in any one place was not an option.

Rather than wasting time while Hok shopped, Ying was keeping himself as busy as his recovering body would allow. Hok had recently purchased a small tarp, and he had just finished rigging it up with branches and rope to create a large canopy over the front half of the skiff. The canopy would block the late-summer sun, as well as the occasional raindrops. It would also provide some protection from the prying eyes of soldiers, who often perched atop bridges along the canal, peering into boats as they passed beneath them.

Ying heard someone approaching, and he quickly adjusted the black silk scarf over his face. He stared upstream, his eyes straining in the dim evening light. He couldn't see very well, so he stood and accidentally bumped his head on the canopy frame.

A moment later, Hok appeared with her herb bag slung over her shoulder. She was wearing a new green dress and matching turban.

Ying relaxed.

"The boat looks different," Hok said. "I like the canopy. Nice work."

"It will take some getting used to," Ying replied, rubbing his head. He pointed to the sides of the skiff. "I also scuffed up the exterior and added a few scratches and gouges. This skiff was too well cared for. Tonglong and his men will never recognize it now."

Hok nodded.

Ying looked Hok's outfit over. "You look different, too. Good idea buying those clothes."

"Thank you," Hok said.

"No luck finding dragon bone?" Ying asked.

Hok shook her head. "It's the strangest thing. Was it always this difficult to locate?"

"Sometimes," Ying said. "Especially in these small villages. Few people can afford it, so few vendors carry it."

"Maybe we should just forget about the dragon bone," Hok suggested.

"Not on your life," Ying replied.

Ying knew that Hok wasn't convinced the small amount of dragon bone they did carry was helping him, but even she could not refute his faster-than-normal healing rate. The herbs she'd been applying to his wounds were certainly part of it, but it seemed something more was helping him quickly regain his strength. Perhaps it was all the extra rest he was getting. Regardless of the reason, in a few days Ying would be more or less back in fighting shape.

Ying thought about the next big city they would come to, the city of Xuzhou. It was located about one-third of the way between the Yellow River and the very end of the Grand Canal at Hangzhou. Xuzhou was where he had had his face carved. The dragon bone he'd carried for much of the past year had come from a vendor in Xuzhou, too. Ying was fairly certain he could find the man again. At the rate they were going, they would be there in four days. He was anxious to get there.

"We should get moving," Ying said.

"I agree," Hok replied. "Let's shove off."

Hok leaned forward to climb into the skiff, and

Ying noticed a green jade crane dangling from a silk thread around her neck. He pointed to it. "You had that in your hand when you escaped the fight club, didn't you?"

"Yes," Hok said.

"Where did you get it?"

"I took it back from General Tsung while we were fighting."

"I mean, where did you get it originally?"

Hok climbed into the skiff and looked away. "I'd rather not talk about it."

"No?" Ying asked, curious. "Not even a little?"

"No."

Ying decided to let it go. He and Hok had traveled in relative silence the entire time. No reason to go and ruin a good thing by asking her a bunch of questions.

Ying jumped out of the skiff onto the bank and gave the boat a big push to free it from the mud. He scrambled back aboard, and they set a course south down the Grand Canal, toward Xuzhou.

Hok took the first shift working the oar. Once they reached the center of the canal, she lashed it in place and let the canal's gentle current carry them downstream. She went over to Ying's side and began to silently rewrap the dressing on his injured shoulder.

Ying watched Hok work. The more she helped him, the less he thought about getting rid of her. She had had plenty of opportunities to take his life, or simply let his life slip away, but she hadn't done so. If she wasn't a threat, perhaps he should just let her remain with him. Of all his former brothers, it seemed it was his sister who might understand him most. It made sense, because she had grown up an outsider, too. First as a girl pretending to be a boy, and now as the pale-skinned, brown-haired daughter of a Chinese woman and a round eye.

Ying looked away. It seemed there were now round eyes everywhere, especially in the large cities. The foreigners brought trade, and trade brought money.

Ying couldn't help but think about Tonglong. Tonglong had a taste for life's finer things and had always admired people with money. Ying had seen it firsthand. Ying recalled how upset Tonglong had been about his burning the map. Ying had never dreamed that Tonglong might have been interested in the dragon scrolls from the very beginning, maybe even before they attacked Cangzhen Temple. Ying had wanted the scrolls so that he could learn dragon-style kung fu. Tonglong had wanted them for other reasons.

Ying assumed that Tonglong must have heard the rumors that floated around the fight clubs about a secret dragon scroll map that led to a dragon's hoard of treasure. Most people assumed that it was a bottomless pile of gold and jewels, but those with more intimate knowledge knew that it was so much more. Beyond an impressive collection of precious metal and stones was supposedly something far more valuable. It was said that the treasure also included four legendary white jade swords and a set of white jade armor. Whoever wielded one of the four swords and also wore the armor was believed to be the rightful heir to the Emperor's throne.

Ying was certain his former brothers and sister knew nothing of these rumors surrounding the dragon scroll map. Otherwise, they would never have shown it to him. While Ying was upset that the remaining dragon training scrolls seemed to be out of his reach, he was hopeful that the treasure would somehow bring him closer to his inner dragon. With the map burned in his memory, all he needed was time to collect it.

An image of Charles suddenly flashed into Ying's mind. Ying wondered how much time would pass before the round eye took action. Charles didn't seem to be the type to sit around long. Without word from Hok, Charles would go looking for her. He probably had a boat and, based on what Ying had seen back at the safe house, he had a lot of friends.

Ying would have to keep an eye out for Charles and any other foreigner. It would be bad enough if Ying accidentally led Tonglong to the treasure. It would be unthinkable for him to lead a foreigner to it.

CHAPTER 17

Charles boarded his sleek sloop behind PawPaw's house, wondering what he was about to get himself into. He set down the last box of supplies beneath the vessel's single mast and stared at the shadow his wide shoulders cast across the deck in the light of the brilliant full moon.

Hok had been gone an entire week, and they hadn't heard a word from her. It was time to take matters into his own hands.

Up the hill, Charles could hear Fu, Malao, and Seh inside PawPaw's house, celebrating the Mid-Autumn Festival. They were eating moon cakes and laughing as PawPaw sang high-pitched, nasally songs and played some sort of traditional stringed instrument that sounded like cats shrieking.

According to Charles' calendar, it was the middle of September, and back in Holland people would be celebrating this Harvest Moon any number of ways. He didn't feel like celebrating anything, though. Not only was Hok missing, he had never quite fit in since bringing Fu, Malao, and Seh here after Tonglong's attack in Jinan. PawPaw was very gracious and he got along just fine with her, but the others hadn't accepted him. They told him that he should have remained with his "foreign" friends back in Jinan.

Charles glanced at the simple Chinese peasant's robe and pants he'd been wearing for weeks. He did look rather silly in them. It was what the locals wore. He didn't enjoy dressing this way; it was simply all he had been able to acquire. He longed to put on a normal shirt and pants. The rough cotton and heavy seams of this robe had rubbed his armpits raw. The only good part about the outfit was the large pocket that formed where the rigid robe cloth met the tight waist sash. It provided him with a place to keep his matching pistols, or "short *qiang*s," as the Chinese called them.

PawPaw's music stopped suddenly, and Charles looked toward the house. He heard Fu growl, low and deep, and then Malao shrieked so sharply it made Charles' yellow hair stand on end. Something wasn't right.

Charles raced up the hill, pulling one of his flintlock pistols from the folds of his robe. He circled around to the front of the house and found the door closed. Usually, it was wide open.

Malao shrieked again.

Without breaking stride, Charles slammed his shoulder into the weathered front door, tearing it from the hinges. The door crashed inward onto the floor, and Charles stumbled in after it. The toe of his boot caught on a piece of splintered doorjamb, and he felt himself hurling toward the floor.

Charles tucked into a tight roll and popped to his feet in one fluid motion. He had performed this roll thousands of times while lion dancing. Instinctively, Charles leveled his pistol, and he found himself aiming at the head of one of the strangest men he'd ever seen. The man had a long torso and curiously short arms and legs. He also had a long, thin mustache that stretched almost to his chest. His nose looked as if it had been beaten flat with an anvil, and he was covered with dirt from head to toe.

Oddest of all was that Charles thought he recognized the man.

"Charles," Seh said, looking in his general direction, "you remember NgGung, don't you? You met him briefly in Kaifeng."

"*Centipede,*" Charles said, lowering his pistol. "Of course, you're one of the bandits. You helped us escape Tonglong's attack during the Dragon Boat Festival. Good to see you again." Charles bowed low, first to NgGung, then to PawPaw. "I am so very sorry. I thought—"

PawPaw laughed. "No need to apologize, Charles. You thought we were in trouble. I might have thought the same thing after those little outbursts you heard." She shook a finger at NgGung. "Our guest here likes to play games. One of his favorites is to sneak into friends' homes and see how long it takes before someone notices him. He didn't get very far this evening with a tiger, a monkey, and a snake keeping me company!"

NgGung shrugged. "You can't blame a guy for trying."

Malao giggled.

NgGung grinned a toothless grin and glanced at Fu, Malao, and Seh. "Excellent work, by the way. An intruder would never get past you three." He stroked his thin, dirty mustache and turned to Charles. "You, on the other hand, my friend, could use a bit of practice in the subtle art of stealthy entry. I do applaud your style, though. It was quite dramatic."

Malao giggled again.

"Uh, thanks," Charles said. "I think." He returned the pistol to the folds of his robe. "So, what are you doing here, NgGung?"

"PawPaw and I have been friends forever," NgGung replied. "I heard a bit of news I thought she might find interesting. I am sure you will, too."

"Hok?" Seh asked.

"That's right," NgGung said. "I've just come from Jinan, where I spoke with a black-market ringleader called HukJee. It seems he is being forced to track Hok for Tonglong."

"I don't understand," Charles said. "If HukJee is working for Tonglong, why would he tell you about it?"

"HukJee is an old friend, too," NgGung said. "He and I do business often. He runs a huge network of black-market vendors who deal in all manner of goods, but they also buy and sell information. They have an elaborate system of runners, who are on the move day and night, keeping the items and information flowing continuously. I am in the information business, too, you know, and HukJee and I trade information like other people trade goods or services. He is a good man, and he doesn't like Tonglong. He told me the details out of frustration."

"Is Hok okay?" Charles asked.

"Perfectly fine, as near as I can tell," NgGung said. "She probably doesn't know she's being tracked, though."

"How is she being tracked?" PawPaw asked.

"Through her shopping habits," NgGung replied. "Hok and Ying have been traveling down the Grand Canal together, searching for dragon bone."

"She's with Ying?" Fu said. "Wait until I get my hands on him—"

"It might not be what you think," NgGung said. "They appear to be working together. Or more likely, Hok is helping Ying. It seems Ying bides his time lying low in their skiff while Hok shops. Unfortunately, all the vendors in this region and beyond have been instructed not to sell her any dragon bone. Sooner or later, Hok will walk into a trap."

"We have to help her!" Malao said.

"Indeed," NgGung said. "I wish I knew how."

"We'll just have to catch up with them," Charles said. "We can do it. I have the fastest boat in all China."

"You mean that foreign sailing vessel at the bottom of the hill?" NgGung asked. "It might be fast on open water, but that tall mast and large sails won't do you any good on the Grand Canal. There is far too much traffic. You would have to row. Also, there are hundreds of low bridges spanning the canal. That mast will never fit under them."

Charles frowned.

Malao scratched his head. "Why are Hok and Ying looking for dragon bone in the first place? I know Ying likes to drink that stuff with fresh snake blood, but what would Hok do with it?"

"I think I can answer that," PawPaw said. "While it might just be a wives' tale, some people believe that dragon bone has special healing properties. Properties that might allow the deaf to hear"—she glanced at Seh—"or the blind to see."

"That's great!" Malao said, slapping Seh on the back. "It sounds like something Hok would do. She's always thinking of others."

Seh paused. "Yes, that sounds like something Hok

would do, but Ying wouldn't. He wanted to abandon me back inside the fight club tunnels because I couldn't see. He is up to something."

"I saw Ying get shot by Tonglong's men," Charles said. "Maybe Hok is treating his injuries."

Seh shook his head. "That might be part of it, but there has to be more. Ying is a loner. I am betting he is afraid to show his face, so he's letting Hok do all the shopping. Hok is probably doing most of the work handling the boat, too. If I know Ying, once he has everything he needs and he feels he can handle the boat alone, he will take it for himself and abandon Hok. NgGung, where were they last spotted?"

"Several *li* north of the city of Xuzhou," NgGung replied.

"How far is that from the end of the Grand Canal?" Seh asked.

"About one-third of the way down," NgGung said. "Why?"

Seh didn't reply.

NgGung grinned. "You're thinking about the dragon scroll map, aren't you? Your father told me about it. He has done some research and believes it leads somewhere far south, perhaps the end of the Grand Canal. Ying is indeed heading in that direction."

"Ying wants the treasure," Fu growled.

"Most likely," NgGung said. "We've learned that Tonglong also wants that map."

"We?" Charles said. "You mean the bandits?"

"Precisely," NgGung said. "Me, Mong, Hung, Gao, Sanfu, plus others you've never met. If we had the resources, we would have sent a team to stop Tonglong from getting his hands on the map. I still remember Tonglong shouting to Seh about the dragon scroll map before he opened fire on you during the Dragon Boat Festival. In hindsight, we probably should have taken the map from Seh for safekeeping."

"The map doesn't matter anymore," Charles said. "I saw Ying burn it out in the center of the Yellow River."

"Ying memorized it, Charles," Seh said. "He has some remarkable skills. He'll know exactly where to go."

"Then we should head south immediately," Charles said. "I know a different route we can take. The Grand Canal ends at the city of Hangzhou, where it spills into the Qiantang River. I've been there. We can take the Yellow River from here all the way to the sea, then follow the coast down to the Qiantang River. From there, we will head up the river to the Grand Canal. My sloop is loaded with supplies and ready to go. She isn't the biggest vessel around, but she is the fastest and can hold the four of us."

"Four of us?" Seh asked.

"That's right," Charles said. "Me, you, Fu, and Malao."

"You want *us* to go with you?" Malao asked. "I

thought all those supplies you were loading into your boat were just for you."

Charles shook his head. "I'll need assistance. You want to help Hok, don't you?"

"Of course," Malao said. "But—"

Fu growled, "Count me in."

"Thank you, Fu," Charles said.

Malao began to fidget. "If Fu is going, I am going, too."

Charles nodded his thanks to Malao.

Seh turned to NgGung. "You mentioned my father. Where is he now?"

"Mong is with the Governor," NgGung replied, "back at the Governor's village. They are making plans."

"What sort of plans?" Charles asked.

"Plans to stop Tonglong," NgGung said. "We believe his ultimate goal is to overthrow the Emperor. While we have no love for the Emperor, we cannot let this happen. It would send the entire country into chaos."

Seh hissed softly. "I want to help stop him."

"We would welcome your assistance," NgGung said. "I am sure Mong would be pleased to have you with us, as would I."

"Will you take me to him?" Seh asked.

"Of course," NgGung answered.

Seh turned to the group. "Fu, Malao, Charles—I hope you will not be disappointed. I will not be joining you."

"What!" Malao said. "You can't leave us, Seh! We need you."

Seh shook his head. "I will only slow you down. Besides, I am not much of a swimmer. I think I can do more good with the bandits."

Fu sighed. "It sounds like they could use you. You are very good at planning things."

Seh nodded.

"Don't go, Seh," Malao said. "Please?"

PawPaw touched Seh's arm. "Go with NgGung. That is the right decision."

Malao pouted.

"All right, Seh," Charles said. "It is decided, then. Fu, Malao, and I will head for Hangzhou. Once we arrive, we will decide whether it's best to wait there for Hok or find a different boat and head up the Grand Canal to track her down. Seh, you will travel with NgGung to the bandits. Once we've found Hok, we will attempt to join back up with you. Agreed?"

"Agreed," Seh said.

Fu, Malao, and NgGung nodded.

PawPaw turned to Charles. "There is a place you should look into once you arrive in Hangzhou. It is a famous apothecary, a shop where people can purchase the very best medicinal herbs. If Hok has made her way that far south, no doubt she will have learned of its existence and will stop in. She is a beautiful young woman with memorable features. I suggest you go there and ask if anyone has seen her."

“Good idea,” Charles said. “I know the place.”

PawPaw smiled and looked at each of the boys in turn. “Don’t any of you forget to come back here and visit me! I am sure NgGung will keep me up to date about your escapades, but it’s always good to see old friends face to face.”

“We will see you again,” Charles said. “That’s a promise. Are we all set, then?”

“Not quite,” Seh said. “We are forgetting about Tonglong. There is a chance he will get to Hok before you do. NgGung, do you have any news of Tonglong’s whereabouts?”

“My sources claim he is headed down the Grand Canal, along with the Emperor and a garrison of soldiers,” NgGung replied. “If I were a betting man, I’d wager that Tonglong was in Xuzhou at this very moment. I’ve heard the city is hosting a special Mid-Autumn Festival fight club event. The Emperor never misses a major fight club event. In fact, I believe your brother Long—I mean, Golden Dragon—is scheduled to fight.”

Malao squawked, “Wait! You said Hok was near Xuzhou!”

NgGung nodded.

“We need to do something right now,” Fu said. “What if she tries to see Long at the fight club?”

“You are already doing everything that can be done,” NgGung said. “All we can do is hope for the best and plan for the worst.” He turned to Charles. “Your plan is a good one.”

"Thank you," Charles said. "I guess as long as Hok and Ying aren't in Xuzhou tonight, they should be fine, right?"

"Right," NgGung said. "There is no point in discussing it further. Let's get you three moving."

CHAPTER 18

Ying and Hok arrived in Xuzhou under the light of a dazzling full moon. The waterway was crowded with travelers vying for dock space, and the canal front buzzed with a carnival-like atmosphere. Colorful lanterns hung everywhere, and the smell of grilled food and moon cake was thick in the night air.

Ying looked over at Hok. “Mid-Autumn Festival,” he said.

Hok nodded.

Remarkably, a slip opened up ahead of them, and Hok eased the skiff in. Ying tied the skiff off, adjusted the black silk scarf across his face, and climbed ashore.

Hok followed, tightening the green turban on her head. She pointed to a posting board farther down the canal front. Even from a distance, Ying recognized that it was a fight club poster. He also recognized the sketch of tonight's featured fighter. It was Long.

"Should we try to see him?" Hok asked.

"No," Ying said. "Too risky. The Xuzhou Fight Club is much more secure than the one in Jinan. There are three times as many guards, and there are sure to be soldiers, too. The Emperor never misses a fight club event here."

Hok tilted her head to one side. "We didn't see the Emperor or his men pass us along the canal."

"We spent a lot of time on the bank with you in the villages. They could have easily passed by without us noticing."

"I suppose," Hok said. "Where is it we are going, then?"

"To the Pet Market," Ying replied.

"Why?"

"I once bought a large supply of dragon bone from a pet vendor here. We'll start with him."

"There is a market for pets?" Hok asked.

"Yes. It has been fashionable for some time here to keep wild animals as pets. The more exotic the pet, the more expensive it is, and the more expensive it is, the more fashionable it is."

"That is unfortunate," Hok said.

Ying shrugged. "It is what it is."

Ying worked his way through the crowd to a series of small, out-of-the-way streets and back alleys. Half an hour later, they arrived at an open-air marketplace.

It was essentially a long, narrow street illuminated by hundreds of oil lamps hung from the eaves of the surrounding buildings. Various vendors had laid out blankets and set up tables, stacking bamboo cages high into the air.

The Pet Market had the feel of a typical outdoor night market but smelled very different. Thousands of animals were on display, each supplying its own assortment of odors, none of them pleasant. For once, Ying's face scarf wasn't such a peculiar sight. Many of the vendors and customers wore them to shield themselves from the horrible smells. There was also a tremendous amount of noise. Birds chirped, cats meowed, and dogs barked. It was as if each animal group was trying to outdo the others.

Everything was represented here, from scales to fur to fins. Some of the animals were in decent shape, but most were not. The majority of creatures were housed in dirty woven-bamboo cages without food or water. Ying saw lizards and snakes of all sizes, their bodies covered in sores, their noses rubbed raw from trying to push their way out of the enclosures. There were rats and monkeys cowering in their own filth, their mange-ridden fur falling out in clumps. Turtles and tortoises were stacked upside down in large pyramids, serving as boundaries between vendor displays. Even Ying, who normally cared little about the welfare of lower life-forms, was uncomfortable.

Hok leaned close to him. "I don't like it here. Please hurry."

Ying nodded and scanned the marketplace. About halfway down the street, he saw the man he was looking for standing next to a gigantic cage filled with hundreds of small, colorful birds.

"Follow me," Ying said, pushing his way into the crowd.

The pet vendor Ying was heading for was a grizzled old man with short, thinning gray hair. His hands were heavily scarred from handling creatures with claws much of his life. Without question, he had the largest collection of exotic creatures in the market. His display contained stack after stack of cages, but it was the sole uncaged creature that captured Ying's full attention. It was an eagle. The bird was not in a cage, but instead was tethered to a large perch.

Ying stared at the enormous bird as he pushed forward. Eagles were powerful, intelligent, and tenacious. They were to be respected, and they were to be feared. Though he would never admit it, if he'd had to pick a kung fu style to learn besides dragon, Ying probably would have picked eagle style.

Sadly, the bird Ying was looking at was dull brown and covered in grime. Many of its feathers had fallen out. Its talons were covered in sores and its eyes were cloudy. It was in horrible condition. Even so, the eagle managed to retain a certain pride and strength that could be felt as well as seen. Ying supposed that was why it was on display. It was likely going to die soon, yet it was clear that when the time came for this eagle to leave the world, it would gladly take *you* along with it.

The pet vendor straightened when he saw Ying and Hok coming. "Good evening," he said with a slight bow.

Ying nodded back. "Good evening. You and I have done business in the past. I am hoping we can do more tonight."

"Excellent," the pet vendor said, clasping his scarred hands. "How can I be of service?"

"I am looking for powdered dragon bone."

The pet vendor paused and looked around, then leaned forward. "Dragon bone, you say? What do you need it for?"

"What difference does it make?" Ying asked.

"I could get in serious trouble for selling it to you."

"Trouble? For selling dragon bone?"

The pet vendor nodded. "The leader of the largest black-market network in the region is prohibiting anyone from selling it, even if they're not in his network—which I'm not. He usually doesn't pay attention to me, and I want it to stay that way. If I sold some and word got out, my days would be numbered."

"I promise not to say a word," Ying said. "How much dragon bone do you have?"

The pet vendor glanced around again. "How much money do you have?"

Ying grasped the coin pouch Charles had given him from HaMo's boat and untied it from his sash. He set it on the small table in front of the man. "This much," Ying said, opening it. He turned to Hok. "What about you?"

Hok was staring at the enormous birdcage. She

replied without looking at him, "I will contribute an equal amount of coins to purchase an equal amount of dragon bone."

The pet vendor's eyes lit up. "Wonderful! I don't keep any here, for obvious reasons, but my supply is not far away. I can retrieve it and be back in less than a quarter of an hour. After I return, we will negotiate specific pricing."

"Good," Ying said. "We're in a hurry."

"I'll leave this instant. Before I go, is there anything else you are considering?"

Ying glanced at the stacks of bamboo cages and smacked his lips. "Yes, a snake or two."

Hok cringed.

"Of course," the pet vendor said. "I have plenty to choose from. How about this Asian vine snake?" He pointed to a snake that appeared to be nearly as long as Ying was tall, but was only as big around as his middle finger.

"Too skinny," Ying replied. He pointed to a very colorful snake with a more robust build. It had a bright blue and black head and looked exactly like Seh's snake. "What is this one?"

"That is a cave-dwelling rat snake. It lives in caves and eats, uh, rats. Bats, too. It's a type of beauty snake."

"It fills its belly with bats and rats?" Ying said. "No thanks. What about these?" He pointed to a large ball of snakes writhing in a small cage. The snakes were black and gray with brilliant yellow triangles and diamonds on their backs.

"Those, my friend, are Mandarin rat snakes. Very beautiful, also."

"I guess," Ying said. "But how do they taste?"

"Excuse me?"

"I asked you how they taste."

"These are . . . ahhh . . . pets."

"So?"

The pet vendor scratched his head. "Well . . . I . . . ummm . . . never mind. Do you want one or not?"

Ying smacked his lips again. "Absolutely."

"Which one?" the pet vendor asked.

Ying thought for a moment. His wounds were healing remarkably fast, and mixing the powdered dragon bone with fresh snake's blood would cure him even faster. However, his left shoulder was quite sore. Wrangling a snake would be a good test to see how far his healing had come.

"Give me the meanest snake you've got," Ying said.

The pet vendor chuckled. He pointed to a small, tightly woven bamboo cage on the ground beneath the table. In it was a snake patterned much like the cave-dwelling rat snake and equally vibrant, but with different coloration. It was primarily yellow in the sections where the cave dweller was blue.

"That is a true beauty snake," the pet vendor said. "I hate that snake. He's more trouble than he is worth. I'll give him to you free of charge if you purchase some dragon bone."

"Perfect," Ying replied.

Hok cleared her throat and turned away from the

birdcage. She knelt in front of the beauty snake's cage and frowned. "He looks amazing."

"Yes, he does," the pet vendor said. "But he's the meanest creature I've ever laid eyes on. Go ahead, get closer."

Hok leaned toward the cage, and the beauty snake reared its colorful head. It opened its mouth, hissing loudly.

Hok stood and backed away, but the snake did not settle down. It kept its eyes locked on Hok.

"Maybe he's just upset that he's in such a small cage," Hok said.

"That's nonsense," the pet vendor replied. "Snakes can't reason. He has plenty of space. Snakes of his type live in cages that size their whole lives and never have any problems. He's just plain mean."

Ying squatted down and put his carved face close to the snake's cage. The snake raised its head even higher and pulled back, forming an *s* shape with its neck. The snake hissed louder and began to vibrate its tail amazingly fast. Ying could feel nervous energy pouring out of the beauty snake, permeating the air around it.

Ying stood and looked at the pet vendor. He grinned. "I'll take it."

"Done!" the pet vendor said with a laugh. "Shall I go get the rest of the merchandise?"

"Yes," Ying replied. He nodded toward the cage with the writhing ball of Mandarin rat snakes. "I'll take them, too."

The pet vendor's eyes widened with delight. "The whole lot?"

Ying nodded. "We can work out a price for them along with the dragon bone." He pointed to a small dagger in the pet vendor's sash. "I'll take that knife, too."

"Sorry," the pet vendor said. "The dagger isn't for sale."

"Do you have knives that are for sale?"

The pet vendor shook his head.

Ying glanced at his fingernails. They were nowhere near as long as they used to be—nor as sharp—but they would probably still work. They would have to do.

"Forget the knife, then," Ying said. "What about a goblet?"

"A goblet?" the pet vendor said. "What do I look like, royalty? I have a drinking bowl, like everybody else." He pointed to a small wooden bowl on the tabletop. "You're welcome to use it. I will return shortly."

"Remember, I'm in a hurry," Ying said.

"Of course," the pet vendor replied. He stepped through the curtain at the back of his booth and disappeared.

Ying grabbed the drinking bowl and heard Hok shuffle her feet.

"You're not going to do what I think you're going to do?" Hok asked. "Are you?"

"I most certainly am," Ying said.

"Well, I can't watch," Hok said.

"Suit yourself," Ying said. "You can go off and look for an additional supplier in case this man does not have enough dragon bone for both of us."

"I think I will," Hok said, scanning the marketplace. "You won't take the dragon bone and leave without me, will you?"

Ying scowled. "Don't insult me like that. I gave you my word that we would do this together."

Hok nodded. "I'll return in a quarter of an hour." She walked away.

"Happy hunting," Ying called out.

Hok didn't reply.

Ying smirked and got to work. He grabbed the pet vendor's drinking bowl, pleased to see that it was empty and, more importantly, clean. He placed the drinking bowl on the edge of the table, then reached down and grabbed the beauty snake's cage. The snake began striking at Ying's hand, trying desperately to bite him through the tight bamboo bars.

Ying admired the tenacity of the creature. It reminded him of himself when he was locked in the Emperor's prison, constantly being taunted and abused by General Tsung. Ying had endured and escaped. This snake, however, would not be so lucky.

Ying set the cage on the ground behind the pet vendor's table. He located the latch on the cage door and opened it. The beauty snake shot forward, its yellow head heading straight for Ying's face.

Ying was ready. He stepped sideways, out of the snake's path, and snapped his right hand outward in an eagle-claw fist. He aimed for the snake's head, but it was too fast. Ying ended up catching the snake by its thin, vibrating tail.

The snake writhed powerfully and twisted around, lunging backward at Ying's hand. Ying snapped his arm out to the side as if he were unfurling his chain whip, and the snake's head was flung harmlessly out of striking range.

After catching hundreds of snakes, Ying had learned that most of them could only strike as far as one-third their body length. By fully extending his arm, he prevented a snake this length from getting to him. It simply wasn't long enough.

On the other hand, Ying could not access enough of the snake's belly from this position. He took a deep breath and grabbed at the snake's midsection with his left hand. Pain from the *qiang* wound shot up through his left shoulder and arm, but he ignored it. His palm made contact with the snake's side, and he latched on to it with a firm grip.

The snake began to writhe even more frantically. It twisted around again, its bright yellow head bearing down on Ying's left hand. Ying let go of the tail with his right hand, reached for the snake's neck, and . . . missed. The snake was too fast. It latched on to the back of Ying's left hand.

Ying fought back a howl. He grabbed at the base of the snake's head with his right hand, but the instant before he made contact, the snake opened its jaws and released its grip. The snake dropped to the ground, slithering powerfully away.

Ying wasn't about to let it escape. He took two long

steps after it, then froze as the creature cruised beneath the curtain and over the tops of four pairs of shoes.

Those shoes hadn't been there a few moments ago.

The curtain parted and Ying saw the pet vendor, smiling from ear to ear. He was flanked by three men, all of whom were carrying *qiang*s pointed directly at Ying.

None of them carried any dragon bone.

CHAPTER 19

"I told you that snake was trouble," the pet vendor said with a laugh. "You should have listened to me, Ying. And you should have been bright enough to know that I would remember you, even with the mask."

Ying scowled. He watched the beauty snake slither beyond the four men and on to freedom. He knew *he* wouldn't get away so easily.

"Put your hands over your head," the pet vendor ordered.

Ying raised his hands, stopping at the black scarf over his face. He adjusted it, stalling for time.

"Leave that mask right where it is," the pet vendor said. "Do not lower it or take it off. I don't want anyone to recognize the latest creature I've captured."

Several passersby saw the armed men and scattered. Ying hated to admit it, but he needed help. He had no chance against three *qiangs*. Perhaps Hok was still near enough that she—

"KEEEEIIIII-AHHHH!" someone shouted, and the sound of splintering bamboo cut through the night air. Ying turned to see Hok smash the gigantic birdcage with her rock-hard elbows and heave a large section of cage at the pet vendor and his three armed accomplices.

The men's arms flew up to protect their faces as hundreds of small, colorful birds rushed toward freedom in a powerful wave of beating wings and thrashing claws.

Hok joined the flock, her elbows and crane-beak fists flying. In the blink of an eye, she disarmed one man and knocked a second unconscious. The third armed man took aim at Hok, and Ying sprang into action.

Ying had his chain whip wrapped around his waist, but there was no time to unfurl it. He ran straight at the man, empty-handed, shrieking with every bit of energy he could muster.

The man spun around, his eyes wide. He centered his *qiang* on Ying's chest and pulled the trigger.

Click!

Ying was close. He launched his right leg forward with a lightning-quick front-kick.

Fizz! BANG!

Ying's foot connected with the *qiang*, swinging the barrel upward. The *qiang* fired just over Ying's head.

His right leg still in the air, Ying pivoted on his left foot and drove his right heel into the man's jaw with a vicious side-kick. The man crumpled.

Ying heard a bloodcurdling shriek and turned to see the eagle straining at its tether, attempting to fly. The *qiang* blast must have frightened it. People throughout the marketplace were screaming and running away.

"Jump back!" Hok shouted.

Ying obeyed without knowing why and saw a flash of metal breeze past his chest. It was the pet vendor's dagger.

The thrown dagger had missed him, but Ying stumbled and lost his balance on a piece of broken birdcage. He crashed into a stack of caged pets. Bamboo snapped, and mice and rats began to scurry free over and around him.

Ying jumped to his feet, brushing the animals away. He heard a man shout and glanced over to see Hok wrestling with the remaining conscious man, who was three times her size. Hok hit him—once—twice—three times—with a crane-beak fist, and he was out.

Ying looked over at the pet vendor and saw that he was reaching for one of the unconscious men's short *qiang*s. Ying untied the chain whip from his waist and lashed out at the *qiang,* knocking it away. The *qiang* stopped next to a monkey's cage, and the skittish creature scooped it up.

The pet vendor froze. So did Ying and Hok. The monkey waved the *qiang* about nervously.

The pet vendor turned his attention to the monkey. He reached out with one hand, saying sweetly, "That's a good boy . . . give it to me . . . I will give you a treat if you behave. . . ." The pet vendor began to walk toward the monkey's cage.

Ying backed away. He saw the pet vendor's dagger among the pile of broken cages and picked it up. He hurried over to the eagle and dropped to his knees, cutting the long tether. The bird spread its gigantic wings and was gone. Ying almost smiled.

"No, no, no!" the pet vendor shouted, and Ying turned to see the man waving his arms frantically. "Don't touch that—"

Click . . . fizz . . . BANG!

The *qiang* erupted and the monkey screeched. A small cloud of dust rose at the pet vendor's feet where the lead ball had buried itself in the ground. Ying watched Hok step through the cloud and rise up on one leg, planting a crane kick in the center of the pet vendor's face. His nose exploded.

The pet vendor howled and fell onto his back from the force of Hok's kick. Ying flew over to the pet vendor's side and raised the dagger high over his head.

"Where is the dragon bone?" Ying hissed.

"Just beyond the curtain!" the pet vendor whined through what was left of his nose. "Take it! All of it!"

Ying eyed him suspiciously.

"I'll get it," Hok offered. "We need to hurry. Soldiers will be coming."

Ying stared hard at the pet vendor. "She is going to go in there. If there are any traps—"

"No traps!" the pet vendor blubbered. "I promise."

Ying nodded to Hok, and she slipped behind the curtain. She returned a moment later with a large silk bag embroidered with golden dragons.

"That's it!" the pet vendor said. "See, no tricks."

Ying spat and poised himself over the pet vendor, raising the dagger even higher.

"Have mercy!" the pet vendor pleaded. "Don't kill me!"

"Give me one good reason why I shouldn't," Ying said.

"One reason?" the pet vendor replied with a nervous grin. "All I need to give you is one *word.*"

"I'm listening," Ying said.

The pet vendor cleared his throat. "Saulong," he said hesitantly.

Ying felt his blood run cold. He tightened his grip on the dagger. "How do you know that name?"

A sly smile spread across the pet vendor's face. "I was there when your father announced it to the camp."

Ying blinked. "You knew my father? I don't believe you. What was his name?"

"Cholong," the pet vendor said. "*Loud Dragon.* He used a chain whip, just like the one in your hand. He also had eyes exactly like yours. Your fire burns deep, young man, just like his did. I suspected who you were when you first came here more than a year ago."

Ying lessened his grip on the dagger and stepped away from the pet vendor. He felt dizzy.

The pet vendor sat up. "It's been a long time, Sau-long."

"Don't call me that," Ying said.

"Okay," the pet vendor said. "Whatever you say, Ying."

"Don't call me that, either!" Ying roared. He began to shake. He felt sweat pouring across his carved fore-head and down his carved cheeks. What was happen-ing to him?

Ying shook his head to clear it. He took a deep breath. So what if this man had known his father? So what if this stranger knew his original name? That was ages ago.

Ying's eyes filled with rage. "My father is dead and my name has been changed. I don't care about the past. Of what use are you to me?"

"If you don't care about the past," the pet vendor said, "then what about the future?"

"What do you mean?" Ying asked.

The pet vendor smiled. "Let me go free and I'll tell you where you can find something far more valuable than dragon bone."

"And that would be?"

The pet vendor's smile broadened. "Your mother."

CHAPTER 20

Tonglong sat in the lap of luxury, his mother at his side. In front of them sat the Emperor with his enormous bodyguard, Xie. They were all lounging together inside the Xuzhou Fight Club, in the Emperor's personal seating area. They had arrived the previous day, exhausted from the long boat ride down the Grand Canal. It was time for some excitement.

Tonglong looked down into the pit arena. He remembered this one well. It was nearly identical to the one at the Jinan Fight Club, a deep, brick-lined hole wide enough to give the combatants plenty of room to maneuver. Off to one side was a single large door that led to a network of underground tunnels.

The door swung open in dramatic fashion, and the

crowd erupted with cheers. The fight club owner announced that they would begin the night with something special. One of the headliners, Golden Dragon, would fight first.

Tonglong had never seen Golden Dragon fight. He was looking forward to this.

Golden Dragon entered the pit arena, and the crowd roared. Bettors began to scramble to and from the bettors' table. Golden Dragon's opponent soon shuffled into the arena, and the crowd jeered. He was an obese foreign round eye with a pale, bald head and hairy back. He was much older, and much larger, than Golden Dragon.

The fight club owner left the pit arena through the tunnel doorway, and the door slammed shut. A huge gong rang out, and the fight began.

Golden Dragon's opponent was twice his size, but it was immediately clear to Tonglong that the huge foreigner wasn't half the fighter Golden Dragon was. Golden Dragon zigged and zagged across the stone floor, mimicking the movements of a mythical dragon with inhuman fluidity. He floated and sank, adjusting his weight to allow for maximum velocity should he decide to strike. He was biding his time, sizing up his lumbering, cumbersome opponent.

Tonglong knew that you could tell a lot about a person by watching him or her fight. Some fighters were constantly on the attack, while others were counterpunchers. Some committed to a technique and followed through, while others primarily used feints.

Some were very technical, while others were brawlers who lived for the lucky punch.

It was said that Golden Dragon was a technical counterpuncher who committed. The hairy foreigner was rumored to be just the opposite. To the uninformed, this might sound like an interesting match. In real life, it was a disaster waiting to happen.

The foreigner quickly grew tired of Golden Dragon's hypnotic movements and dropped his hands, running straight at Golden Dragon, attempting to tackle him. Golden Dragon backed up to the perimeter wall and sank low, then rose high into the air with a powerful leap that took him clear over the foreigner. Unable to stop his own forward momentum, the foreigner crashed into the solid brick wall with a loud *THUD!*

The crowd roared with laughter.

Tonglong was not amused. He'd noticed that Golden Dragon had had the perfect opportunity to kick his opponent in the head as he flew over, which would have inflicted significant damage. However, Golden Dragon had held back. Allowing a fight to continue a moment longer than necessary could mean the difference between life and death. Golden Dragon was intelligent enough to know this. He was up to something.

The foreigner turned to face Golden Dragon.

Again, Golden Dragon sank low.

The foreigner rushed toward Golden Dragon, and Golden Dragon unleashed a powerful roundhouse kick. Tonglong could clearly see the momentum build from Golden Dragon's foot, up through his leg, into his hip, and around his waist—then back out the same way, like a dragon whipping its tail. The kick should have cracked the foreigner's skull in two. Instead, Golden Dragon's foot only grazed the burly man's forehead, stunning him.

The crowd gasped.

Tonglong's eyes narrowed. It took incredible skill and precision to graze someone's head like that.

The foreigner wobbled, and the crowd began to chant, "Finish him! Finish him! Finish him!"

Golden Dragon's jaw tightened visibly. Tonglong watched him cock back his right arm, form a dragon fist, and let it fly. The raised middle-finger knuckle of Golden Dragon's fist bounced off the side of the foreigner's head, and the big man crashed to the ground, out like a flame in a windstorm.

The crowd roared its approval.

Tonglong shook his head. These peasants had no idea what had just happened. Golden Dragon could have finished the foreigner any number of ways—for good—but instead he'd simply knocked the man out.

Tonglong leaned toward his mother. "Did you see that?" he whispered.

"Yesss," AnGangseh replied. "The boy did not wish to harm his opponent. There is sssomething about that child I do not trust."

"Me neither," Tonglong said. "We must keep an eye on him."

“Agreed,” AnGangseh said.

The Emperor leaned his regal head back toward Tonglong. “Discussing anything interesting?”

“Just commenting on the boy’s extraordinary ssskill, Your Highness.”

“Indeed,” the Emperor said with a sniff. “He has a bright future ahead of him.” The Emperor turned away.

There were a few more fights scheduled for the night, but Tonglong was beginning to feel restless. Not long ago, he had received reports that Ying and Hok had been sighted walking along the canal front right here in Xuzhou. They were moving quickly and had managed to slip away through the crowd before Tonglong’s men could react. However, Tonglong was confident Ying and Hok would be found. It was just a matter of time.

As though it were a sign from the heavens, AnGangseh tapped Tonglong gently on the knee and pointed discreetly toward the fight club’s main door.

Tonglong looked over to see a very excited soldier in the doorway. The man signaled for Tonglong to join him. Tonglong could tell from the soldier’s expression what news he possessed.

Ying had been sighted again.

Tonglong excused himself and headed for the entrance.

CHAPTER 21

Ying pushed his way through Xuzhou's narrow backstreets, light-headed and dizzy. He felt as if he needed to throw up. Hok hurried behind him, carrying the bag of powdered dragon bone they'd taken from the pet vendor, along with Ying's bag of coins, plus her own. They'd been running for more than an hour, but the pet vendor's words still rang clearly in Ying's head. He'd spoken with the man for less than a quarter of an hour, but he knew that that short conversation had changed his life forever.

"Slow down, Ying," Hok said. "The danger is behind us. You should rest and try to clear your head. Trust me, I know what you are going through."

Ying stopped and turned to Hok. He was breathing

heavily, his bruised ribs and injured shoulder screaming at him every time he inhaled. "You don't know a thing about what I'm going through."

"Ying, please—"

Ying snatched his bag of coins from Hok and walked away, adjusting the scarf across his face. He saw an ancient woman ahead, hunched over a small basket that had steam pouring out of the top and hot coals beneath it. Dinner buns. Good. Some food might make his dizziness go away. He approached the old woman and bought everything she had—three buns filled with chicken and three with sweet red-bean paste. After paying, Ying shoved the bean-paste buns at his vegetarian former sister. "Stay close to me and keep your mouth shut," he said.

Ying continued on and soon found a small, out-of-the-way alley off a dark section of street. Even the brilliant moon's rays couldn't reach into its depths. Ying sat down and took a huge bite of dinner bun. It was rather flavorless, but at least it was warm and filling. He had hoped to finish it in peace and quiet, but it seemed Hok had other plans.

"We need to talk," Hok said.

"I have nothing to say to you," Ying replied.

"You've just been through a lot," Hok said. "Let me help you."

Ying didn't respond.

"The pet vendor said that your mother lives at the end of the Grand Canal," Hok said. "Let's go there."

"What makes you think I want to see her?"

"I would want to see *my* mother."

"I thought you came on this trip to help Seh."

"I did, but I don't think Seh will be any worse off if I wait a few extra weeks, or even longer, to begin giving him powdered dragon bone as a treatment. Let me help you first."

Ying noticed that his hands were still shaking. He curled back his upper lip, angry that Hok was pushing him and upset that she was seeing him like this. "Why do you keep wanting to help me? Don't say that's just what people do. I don't buy it."

"People should help one another," Hok said, "and you obviously could use some help. It's that simple. You can accept my words or disregard them. Believe what you want to believe. That's what you're going to do, anyway."

"What do you mean by that?"

"You've never listened to anyone, no matter how good the advice."

"That's because most people are stupid."

Hok stared, unblinking, at him. "You are very clever, Ying. No one will deny that. However, just because you are smarter than most people does not mean that most people are stupid."

"Leave me alone."

"No."

Ying took another bite of his dinner bun. "I hate you," he mumbled.

"I realize that. After all, you tried to kill me and the

others," Hok said matter-of-factly. "Oddly enough, I never understood why it is you hate us so much."

"Because you were spoiled rotten," Ying said.

"You wanted to kill us because you were jealous of us?"

"That's not what I said."

"Yes, it is."

"Grandmaster treated all of you differently than me," Ying said. "He treated *you* differently, even though you were no more special than I was. In fact, I'm better at kung fu than any of you. I worked harder than any of you. I went on a mission for Grandmaster, and I never received any recognition for it. I even lost my best friend on that mission. It was so . . . unfair."

"Sounds like jealousy to me."

Ying spat and glared at Hok, but she wouldn't let it go.

"I had no control over how Grandmaster treated you," Hok said. "Neither did any of the others. For you to take it out on us, that's unfair."

"You could have stood up for me," Ying said.

"How do you know that I didn't?"

"Don't be ridiculous," Ying said. "I never heard you utter a single word in my defense."

"That doesn't mean that I remained silent. I stood up for you many times."

"Give me one example."

"Remember the time I spent an entire week scrubbing the floor of every building within the Cangzhen compound? I distinctly remember you mocking me for days."

Ying thought back. "Yes, I suppose I do."

"Do you remember what you did the day before I started scrubbing?"

"No, I . . . wait a moment, yes," Ying said. "Grandmaster made a big fuss about me hiding down in the escape tunnels. It was the first time Fu had woken me. I attacked Fu."

"That's right," Hok said. "I told Grandmaster that Fu should never have done that. Everyone knows how you react when you're woken without warning, including Fu. I told Grandmaster that punishing you was unfair. You weren't bothering anyone by going into the tunnel. Fu was bothering *you*."

Ying stared at Hok, dumbfounded. "You said that to Grandmaster? How did he respond?"

"He got really angry at me, of course. He told me I was the one who should mind her own business. Scrubbing the floors was my punishment."

"How come you never told me this?"

"What difference would it have made?"

"A lot. I would have known that you were on my side."

"So, if a person is not openly fighting for you, then he or she is against you?" Hok asked.

"I . . . I don't know," Ying said.

"I think you do know," Hok said. "You need to rethink how you think everybody else thinks. For someone so smart, you sure can be stupid. Most people are neither for you nor against you. They have too many other things to worry about in their own lives. They don't have time to spend wondering about your situation. Don't flatter yourself so much."

Ying didn't know what to say. He was beginning to feel dizzy again. He lifted his hand to take another bite out of his dinner bun when a small boy suddenly darted out of the alley's darkest corner. The child managed to grab Hok's and Ying's bags of coins before Ying even thought to act.

As the boy scurried away, Ying dove at him, catching the boy by one scrawny ankle. The boy squealed and squirmed as Ying clamped down hard with an eagle-claw grip, compressing skin, muscle, and tendon. The boy yelped, tears welling up in his dirty eyes. He dropped the bags of coins.

Hok stood. "Let him go, Ying."

"I don't think so," Ying replied. "Nobody takes what's mine. I'm going to teach him a lesson."

"You've hurt him plenty," Hok said. "He's just a little boy and he's probably starving to death. Look how skinny he is. Take the coins back and give him a bun."

"No," Ying said. "I'm not in the mood for charity. He took my coins with his right hand, so I am going to break that hand for him." Ying reached out for the boy's tiny hand.

"I'm warning you, Ying. Don't harm him."

Ying could see the seriousness in Hok's eyes. After seeing the damage she did back at the pet market, Ying wasn't sure he wanted to tangle with her tonight. He pulled his free hand away from the boy and slightly loosened his eagle-claw grip on the boy's ankle. The kid stopped crying, and Hok sat back down.

Hok sighed. "Please just let him go, Ying. I'm tired of arguing with you. He can even take my coins if he truly thinks he needs them more than I do."

"Have you lost your mind?" Ying said. "You'd let him take your money?"

Hok nodded. "It looks like he's in a worse situation than you or me. I bet he has no family. No home. No food." She looked at the boy. "Is that true?"

The boy nodded, sniffling.

"See," Hok said.

"So what?" Ying replied. "I was an orphan, too."

Hok gave him a disgusted look. "Give me a break, Ying. You always had food on your table, a roof over your head, and clothes on your back."

Ying ground his teeth but said nothing.

Hok looked at the boy. "What is your name?"

"ShaoShu," he replied.

"Little Mouse?" Hok asked.

The boy nodded.

Ying snorted. "It's fitting."

Hok ignored his comment. "Did your parents give you that name?"

"I don't remember who gave me that name," ShaoShu replied in a small voice. "That is the only thing anyone has ever called me. Well, that and some curse words."

Ying smirked. "Imagine that."

Hok glared at Ying. "Give him a break. I bet ShaoShu would feel terrible stealing from us if he knew our situation."

"Don't be ridiculous," Ying said. "He is a little thief. He doesn't care about you or me. He only cares about himself."

"That's funny," Hok said. "Sounds like somebody else I know."

Ying hissed loudly and stood, releasing ShaoShu. "That's it," Ying said. "I've had it. This conversation is over. I'm leaving."

"Me too," ShaoShu squeaked. He shoved a dinner bun in his mouth and scurried away.

Ying watched ShaoShu go and smiled. He pointed to the large bag jingling in ShaoShu's left hand.

"ShaoShu!" Hok called out. "My coin bag! Bring it back! Running off like this isn't the right thing to do! Not until we finish talking. Don't make me look like a fool!"

ShaoShu rounded a corner and was gone.

Ying snickered. "He certainly did make you look like a fool."

Hok pointed toward Ying's feet. "Is that so? Then what did he make you out to be?"

Ying looked down and ground his teeth. ShaoShu had somehow managed to steal his coin bag, too.

"Why, that little—" Ying began to say.

"Get over it, Saulong," Hok interrupted in an aggressive tone. "We still have your precious dragon bone."

Ying froze and his eyes darkened. "What did you call me? Don't ever use that name again."

"Why not?" Hok asked. "You've never been happy with the name *Eagle. Vengeful Dragon* suits you perfectly."

"I'm warning you, Hok. You have no idea what it's like to have had your name changed."

Hok surprised him with a shrill laugh. "You never cease to amaze me, Ying. What makes you think you are the only one with a different name?"

Ying didn't reply.

"That's right," Hok said. "I had a different name, too. Except I also had to shave my head and dress like a boy every day for nine years. How many times did *you* have to put on a turban and dress like a girl to hide your true nature?"

Ying said nothing.

"That's what I thought," Hok said. "You never had to do it. Not even once. Complaining about your life doesn't do you any good. Get over yourself."

Ying frowned. His head ached. He needed to get away from Hok, but she continued to push him.

"Let's talk about your mother," Hok said.

"No."

"Come on, Ying," Hok said, her voice softening. "It will help you. I've been through this." She pulled the tiny jade crane out from behind the collar of her dress. "You asked me about this earlier. My mother gave it to me before she took me to Cangzhen. I remember it like it was yesterday."

Ying didn't respond.

"Trust me, Ying," Hok said. "I can help."

"I trust no one," Ying replied.

Hok shook her head and sighed. "I think that might be your biggest problem."

"I don't want to talk about it."

"Of course you don't," Hok said. "You want to run away like you always do. Either that, or you want to smash something. Running and smashing solve nothing, Ying."

"Stop talking!" Ying shouted. He clenched his fists and bit his lip, his pointed teeth drawing blood. He needed to go. Another shout like that and he'd draw unwelcome attention to himself. Ying grabbed the bag of powdered dragon bone and tore the turban from Hok's head.

Hok didn't budge.

Ying unrolled the turban and poured half the dragon bone in a pile in the center of it. He scowled at Hok. "You may know a thing or two about me, but you know nothing about my mother. I put my trust in her, and she abandoned me. Everything I know about trust I learned from her and Grandmaster."

"Do you want me to come with you when you go to find her?" Hok asked.

Ying didn't reply. He rolled Hok's turban around her share of the dragon bone and handed it to her.

"How do you know that the directions the pet vendor gave you were accurate?" Hok asked. "He could have been lying."

"He was telling the truth," Ying said.

"You trust *him*?"

"No, I don't trust him. But I believe him."

"Why?"

"Because the directions that he gave me aligned perfectly with the dragon scroll map in my head," Ying said. "That can't be coincidence. Goodbye, Hok. Find someone else to take care of."

Ying turned and walked quickly away.

CHAPTER 22

For the next half hour, Ying clung to the shadows, snaking his way in and out of Xuzhou's blackest alleyways. Traveling this way would make him take much longer to return to the skiff, but at least he could make certain he wasn't being followed. After the skirmish with the pet vendor and his argument with Hok, he couldn't be too careful. Especially in his state of mind.

Hok had nearly driven him mad. Who did she think she was, talking to him that way? She had spoken to him as if he were a child. She had acted as if she were his parent, as if she were in control. He would show her who was in control. He was taking the skiff. Hok could find her own way home.

Ying was almost to the canal front when something heavy dropped from the sky. It crashed in front of his feet. It appeared to be a bag of coins. In fact, it appeared to be *his* bag of coins.

Ying heard jingling overhead and looked skyward. A second bag of coins came plummeting down, landing next to the first bag. It was Hok's bag.

ShaoShu, Ying thought.

"Show your face!" Ying hissed.

ShaoShu's tiny head appeared over the edge of the rooftop directly above Ying. The boy was silhouetted by the bright moonlight.

Ying pointed to the coin bags. "What is this about?"

"I thought about what your friend said," ShaoShu replied. "She is right. Stealing is wrong. Keep your stupid coins."

Ying's carved eyebrows rose. "This had better not be a trick, you little rodent. If these bags are poisoned, I will hunt you down and—"

"No tricks," ShaoShu said. "I promise."

Ying eyed the boy suspiciously. "You're returning these simply because you feel bad?"

"I didn't exactly feel bad taking them from you," ShaoShu said, "but I feel bad taking them from her."

Ying scowled at the boy. "What about my dinner bun?"

"I ate it," ShaoShu replied. "But I don't feel bad about that. I have some news for you that is worth a whole lot more than a dinner bun. Someone called

General Tonglong is here in Xuzhou. He has men hiding in boats all along the canal, waiting to catch you."

Ying stared up at ShaoShu. "Who told you this?"

"I overheard two soldiers talking about it. They said they were going to capture you and then kill you. Your friend, too."

"Why are you telling me these things?" Ying asked.

ShaoShu shrugged, his little shoulders rising over the roof's edge. "Because it's the right thing to do."

Ying scoffed. "How did you know I would be passing through this alleyway?"

"This is the way I would have come if I wanted to stay out of everyone's sight," ShaoShu said. "This is the closest alley to the canal front."

"How did you get here before me?"

"Shortcuts. I know a million of them."

"So, you know the city streets well?"

"Better than anyone," ShaoShu said.

"What about the canal?" Ying asked. "Can you handle a boat?"

"I know the canal as well as the streets, and I can handle a boat. I've, uh, borrowed one or two before."

Ying smirked. He might just have a way out of here yet. "If I describe a certain skiff to you and tell you where it is docked, do you think you could take it down the canal for me?"

"Sure," ShaoShu said. "But why would I?"

Ying picked up his bag of coins. "Because I'll give you half of these."

"It's a deal!" ShaoShu said.

"Good," Ying said. "Is there a spot downriver that I can walk to quickly in relative security and you can travel to in the skiff?"

"Yes," ShaoShu replied. "I know the perfect place. There is a fancy park about two *li* downstream from where we are now. You can follow side streets and alleys south along the canal until you reach it. There is an old elm tree on this side of the canal that hangs low over the water. I will take the skiff down the canal and beach it under the tree for you."

Ying looked up at him. "Where will you be?"

"Inside the skiff, waiting for you."

"Why?"

ShaoShu looked confused. "Because I'm coming with you."

Ying's carved brow rose. "No, you're not."

"Yes, I am," ShaoShu said, "or I'm not going to help you. I hate it here. I want to go somewhere else."

"Well, you aren't staying with me."

"I won't stay with you. You are mean. I'll find a dry corner in some other city, just like I had here. I only want a ride out of here."

Ying gave up. "Fine. Are you sure I can trust you to deliver the skiff to the park?"

"Of course," ShaoShu said. "I have to trust you, too, you know. You're the one who wanted to break my hand."

Ying nodded. He had a point. "All right, then. Let's get on with it." Ying turned to walk away.

"Hey, where are you going?" ShaoShu asked.

Ying looked up at him as if he were crazy. "To the park."

ShaoShu's eyes widened with surprise. "What about your friend?"

"What about her?"

"Isn't she going, too?"

"No."

"You are just going to leave her here?" ShaoShu said. "You can't. The soldiers are looking for her, too. I told you that." He glared at Ying.

Ying lowered his head and rubbed his temples. His headache was coming back. "All right, you go get the skiff and head downstream. I'll go find her."

ShaoShu didn't reply.

Ying looked up and saw that ShaoShu was staring farther back into the alley, over Ying's shoulder. Ying spun around and was shocked to see Hok walking silently toward him.

"How did you find me?" Ying asked her.

"I have been following you," Hok replied. "You are very good at traveling undetected, but I am better."

Ying frowned. "How long have you been standing back there?"

"Long enough," Hok said. She locked eyes with him. "I am glad that you decided to look for me. Thank you."

Ying looked away. He didn't know what to say.

"The polite response would be 'You're welcome,' " Hok said.

Ying shuffled his feet and looked at her. "You're welcome."

Hok nodded and looked up at ShaoShu. "My name is Hok, ShaoShu, and his name is Ying. Do as he said and go get the skiff now. We will meet you downstream as you suggested. Hurry."

CHAPTER 23

At daybreak, Ying and Hok found ShaoShu right where he said he would be, with the skiff. Except for a few elderly individuals exercising, they had the entire park to themselves. ShaoShu looked at Ying, and a huge grin spread across the boy's face.

"What?" Ying asked.

"I told you that you could trust me," ShaoShu said.

"I suppose you are right," Ying said. "I'll keep my end of the bargain, too, to show that you can trust me. You may remain with us. Just make sure you stay out of the way."

"You won't even know I'm here," ShaoShu said. "Thank you."

Ying nodded.

Hok turned to Ying. "Where to?"

"We will head south," Ying replied.

"How far?" ShaoShu asked.

"To the end of the Grand Canal, just beyond the city of Hangzhou."

"Wow!" ShaoShu said. "I've always wanted to go there. Are we going to meet someone?"

Ying paused and looked at ShaoShu. "We need to get something straight right now. Hok doesn't talk much, and I talk even less. If you are going to travel with us, you're going to have to keep your mouth shut. No more questions."

ShaoShu made a gesture as if he were locking his mouth and throwing away the key.

"I am serious," Ying said.

ShaoShu nodded back, silent. He suddenly seemed serious, too. Very serious.

Ying rubbed his carved chin and turned away. Perhaps there was more to ShaoShu than met the eye.

They shoved off, with Hok taking the first shift on the oar and Ying and ShaoShu under cover beneath the skiff's canopy. Their plan was to travel continuously, stopping only long enough to stock up on basic supplies such as food. Hok would not try to find any additional herbs for her medicine bag. They hoped that as long as they kept moving, Tonglong would not catch them.

Ying and Hok soon settled into a routine similar to the one that they had established heading to Xuzhou, with ShaoShu constantly on the lookout for trouble.

They were running with the current, so rowing wasn't much of a chore. Ying and Hok took turns, with Hok taking many of the daylight hours. Ying got plenty of rest, and that, plus the new dragon bone—at least in his opinion—helped get his sore shoulder quickly back on the mend.

True to his word, ShaoShu kept quiet. So much so that Ying had to look at him whenever he asked the boy a question because ShaoShu would often reply with only a head shake or a nod. ShaoShu spent hour after hour silently staring at the world around them, seemingly soaking it all in. Ying spent a lot of time beneath the canopy with ShaoShu, but somehow Ying hardly noticed the small boy. He had a way of disappearing right under Ying's nose. ShaoShu seemed to enjoy curling into a tight ball and hiding in the most impossible places, even on this tiny boat. Ying found he didn't mind having the kid around at all.

As the days passed, their surroundings changed from forest to farmland to village and back to forest, in no particular order. The late-summer weather changed often, too. It would be raining heavily one moment, then sunny and hot the next, followed by a chilly day.

The only constant Ying noticed was an odd one. Early every morning, no matter where they were, if it wasn't raining, he saw old people exercising along the canal like the ones he'd seen at the park in Xuzhou. He assumed they were practicing something called *Tai Chi Chuan,* or Grand Ultimate Fist. He had never seen *Tai Chi* before, but he'd heard of it. He'd found the name amusing because it appeared to be nothing more than a series of slow-motion exercises that old people used to stay in shape. He knew that breathing techniques played an important part, and he could hear some of the practitioners hacking and wheezing as if they were taking their last breaths. On a couple of occasions, he half expected Hok to have to jump out and attend to the old-timers. There was nothing grand or ultimate or even fistlike about any of it.

Things went smoothly until they reached the city of Zhenjiang a week later. Zhenjiang was built on the banks of the mighty Yangtze River. The Yangtze was so famous, Ying had learned of it back at Cangzhen Temple. It was said that the Yangtze was even bigger than the Yellow River. Once Ying laid eyes on the extraordinarily wide Yangtze, he believed it. Unfortunately, before they would be allowed to cross it to continue down the Grand Canal, they had to pass through a check station.

Ying had heard about check stations, but this was his first time passing through one. They were set up by the Emperor's men or regional warlords to assist with manhunts. Ying had a feeling he knew who this check station had been set up to intercept.

Ying was working the skiff's oar, and he called out to Hok in a hushed tone, "You're going to have to take the oar. There is a check station ahead. I have to hide, and you have to figure out a way to not look like yourself. Pretend you have buckteeth or something."

“But there isn’t any place to hide someone your size on this skiff,” Hok said. “We don’t have blankets or anything like that—”

“Blankets are no good,” ShaoShu interrupted. “Everybody hides beneath blankets. I’ll show you how to hide. Lie down under the canopy, Ying. I’m going to make a junk pile around you.”

Ying hesitated.

“Don’t you trust me?” ShaoShu asked. “You said you did.”

Ying hesitated another moment, then handed the oar over to Hok. He hurried beneath the canopy and cleared a space on the floor of the skiff, then lay down.

ShaoShu stepped next to him. “Give me your socks,” he said.

“My socks?” Ying asked.

ShaoShu nodded. “The ones you’re wearing right now. Nothing keeps nosy people away from junk piles better than dirty socks. I’ll let you borrow mine, too, if you want.”

“Wonderful,” Ying said, making a sour face. He removed his shoes and socks and handed both to ShaoShu.

ShaoShu took only the socks. “Keep your shoes hidden close to you or put them back on,” he said. “They are too big to be Hok’s or mine. They will look suspicious on top of the pile.”

Ying smiled. ShaoShu was good.

ShaoShu went to work, grabbing food, rope, the skiff’s push pole—anything that wasn’t tied down.

In a matter of moments, Ying found himself expertly buried, invisible to the world.

Ying lay there for nearly an hour before he finally heard soldiers asking questions of travelers. They were about to pass through the check station. He felt the skiff bump against a dock, and the pile shifted slightly. Ying noticed a sliver of light near his right eye, and he tilted his head, aligning his eye with it. A small gap had formed in the pile, and Ying could see out of it. He saw that the skiff had been pulled alongside a makeshift dock, and there was a soldier standing on the dock, near the skiff's stern. The soldier did not look happy.

CHAPTER 24

"What are your names?" the soldier asked.

From beneath the pile, Ying heard Hok say, "My name is Ming, and this is my little brother, Ching."

"Ming and Ching?" the soldier said. "Hmmm. Where are you heading?"

"We are traveling south to the city of Wuxi," Hok lied. "We would like to cross the famed Yangtze River here, if that is okay with you."

"You two appear harmless enough," the soldier said, appearing to relax. "I just need to search your skiff, and you can be on your way."

"Search the skiff?" Hok said. "Whatever for?"

"Oddly enough, we're looking for a girl whose description vaguely matches you. However, our target has, ah, different teeth and is traveling with a male who is older than she is, not younger. The male is a teenager and his face is carved to resemble a dragon. You haven't seen a young teenage man with a dragon's face, have you?"

"A dragon's face?" Hok replied. "Heavens, no. Dragons scare me."

"Me too!" ShaoShu squeaked.

Beneath the pile, Ying stifled a laugh.

"This will only take a moment," the soldier said, and Ying felt the skiff rock as the man climbed aboard. "I just need to poke through that pile under your canopy, and you can be on your way."

Ying no longer felt like laughing. His blood ran cold.

"Excuse me," ShaoShu said. "Can I help? When I grow up, I want to be a soldier, just like you."

The soldier laughed. "You want to be a soldier, huh? Well, sure, you can help. Come on over here."

Ying frowned. What was ShaoShu up to? He heard ShaoShu say, "Thanks!" and felt a thud as ShaoShu jumped on top of the pile.

"Whoa!" ShaoShu called out, and Ying felt the pile begin to shift. "Help me!" ShaoShu cried. "I'm falling and I can't swim—"

ShaoShu's words were cut short by a loud *splash!* The gap in the pile near Ying's eye had opened a bit more, and Ying saw ShaoShu flailing in the water a surprising distance from the skiff.

"Somebody, please, help him!" Hok cried, playing along. "I can't swim, either."

Ying heard the soldier grunt, and the skiff rocked as the man dove into the canal. Ying saw the soldier swim over to ShaoShu, grab him by the collar, and haul him back toward the skiff. The soldier must have been a powerful swimmer because he managed to lift ShaoShu out of the water and drop him into the skiff. The soldier then swam over to the dock and climbed out of the canal. He stood, dripping wet, and scolded ShaoShu.

"You two have no business traveling by boat if you cannot swim!" the soldier said. "Now move along, I've got real work to do."

Ying heard Hok take hold of the oar, and they pulled quickly away from the dock. He remained hidden until ShaoShu poked his tiny head into the pile nearly an hour later. They were most of the way across the wide Yangtze River by that time.

"Are you okay?" ShaoShu asked. "I hope I didn't hurt you when I jumped onto the pile. It was the only thing I could think of."

"Hurt me?" Ying said. "I'm fine. That was some fast thinking, ShaoShu. I'm impressed. One question, though—do you really not know how to swim?"

"Of course I know how to swim," ShaoShu replied. "I might be a little crazy sometimes, but I'm not stupid."

Ying smiled. "Very well. Thank you, ShaoShu. I'm glad I trusted you."

"Me too," Hok added from the stern.

ShaoShu blushed. "Do you want me to dig you out now?"

Ying shook his head. "I think I'd better stay under here awhile longer, just to be safe. Would you mind covering me back up?"

ShaoShu nodded and went to work without saying another word.

South of the Yangtze River, the current in the Grand Canal was much stronger and continued to work in their favor. The canal also widened substantially. There were many more stone bridges and pagodas in this region, along with increasingly larger villages. As they continued south, day after day, the villages soon became cities and Ying began to feel claustrophobic. There were people and boats everywhere, and many more locks. He ended up wearing his black silk mask at all hours, hating every moment of it. He even hid beneath ShaoShu's junk pile on a few occasions, though they didn't encounter any more check stations, fortunately.

The canal eventually passed through the city of Wuxi, the fake destination Hok had given the soldier, and continued around the eastern edge of the gigantic Lake Tai. They passed through the city of Jiaxing, where there was another fight club, and Ying knew they were getting close. Finally, more than two weeks after leaving Xuzhou, they reached the bustling city of Hangzhou.

The Grand Canal was more crowded here than anywhere Ying had ever been in his life. Boats were being loaded and unloaded everywhere he looked. The sea was close by, and Hangzhou was the main hub where goods from all over China—and beyond—were exchanged. Ying saw more round eyes than he could count. The closer they got to the center of the city, the more round eyes he saw. They were everywhere.

Ying thought about Charles. He would probably feel right at home here. Ying, on the other hand, didn't like it one bit. He turned to Hok. "See anybody you know?" he joked.

Hok shot him an irritated glance.

"Yeah, me neither," Ying said. "They all look the same to me."

Hok shook her head.

They continued on, passing through the congestion of central Hangzhou to the southern edge of the city. Here, the canal ended, emptying into the Qiantang River.

"Are we almost there?" ShaoShu asked.

"Yes," Ying replied. He turned to Hok, who was working the oar. "According to the pet vendor, we need to follow the river west, toward the sea, for several hours until we see a small tributary branching south that is flanked by twin pagodas. We're supposed to follow that for another *li* or so until we come upon a tidy house set far from the water at the base of a steep, tree-covered hill."

"Are you nervous?" Hok asked.

Ying didn't answer.

Hok glanced at ShaoShu, then back at Ying. "If you want to go alone, I understand. I have enough money to stay here in Hangzhou."

Ying thought for a moment. "I'll let you know," he said.

Hok turned the boat onto the river and felt the canal's current subside and the river's current begin to pull them west, toward the sea. Ying scanned the riverbank. Docked along the wide river were huge foreign sailing vessels and smaller seafaring Chinese junks. Workers of various races hurried in every direction, loading and unloading goods. Ying turned to say something to Hok but saw that her eyes were fixed on a gigantic storefront.

Ying read the enormous sign. It was an apothecary. He couldn't imagine how many different medicinal herbs were housed in a building that size. "I bet you could spend hours in that place," he said.

Hok grinned. "Days, probably."

Ying paused. "Why don't you, then? The more I think about it, the more I'd rather continue on alone. I'll come back in a few days."

"Are you sure?" Hok asked.

Ying nodded.

"What are you two talking about?" ShaoShu asked.

"Ying needs to go someplace alone," Hok said. "We will dock soon. I am going to stay here at an inn. What are you going to do?"

"Can I stay with you?" ShaoShu asked.

"Of course," Hok replied. "You can stay with me as long as you'd like."

"Thank you!" ShaoShu said. "Thank you, thank you, thank you! You and Ying are the nicest people in the world!"

Ying felt his cheeks begin to blush. He looked away.

"Am I really going to stay in an inn?" ShaoShu asked Hok.

"Yes," Hok replied. "One that serves meals and has hot baths."

"Hurray!" ShaoShu said. "I've never had a hot bath before. Where are you going, Ying?"

Ying looked at ShaoShu. "To find my mother."

"Really?" ShaoShu asked. "Are you excited?"

"No questions," Ying replied, half joking. "Remember?"

"Sorry," ShaoShu said, and again he pretended to lock his mouth closed.

Ying nodded, and Hok turned the skiff toward the apothecary. She found an unoccupied slip among the docks out front and pulled in. Ying grabbed hold of a dock pylon, and Hok and ShaoShu climbed out.

Hok slipped her herb bag over her shoulder and tightened the green turban on her head. "When and where should we meet again?" she asked.

"We can meet right here," Ying replied. "This is a busy area. You should be able to find an inn nearby."

Hok nodded. "How long will you be gone?"

"I'm not sure," Ying replied. "I don't know how long it will take to get there, and I should probably spend some time with her. How about three days?"

"Three days sounds good," Hok said. "Let's meet here at sunset."

Ying nodded and glanced at ShaoShu. "I almost forgot something important," Ying said. "Hok, open your medicine bag, please."

Hok gave Ying a quizzical glance but did as he asked. Ying untied his bag of coins from his sash with one hand and dumped half the contents into Hok's medicine bag.

"You did well, ShaoShu," Ying said. "You deserve this."

ShaoShu grinned but didn't say a word, his mouth still locked closed.

"You can talk now," Ying said.

"I'm rich!" ShaoShu squealed. "Thank you!"

Ying smiled. As much as he hated to admit it, he was going to miss *Little Mouse.* "Take care of Hok while I'm gone, okay?" he said.

ShaoShu suddenly grew serious. "I will guard her with my life," he said. Ying didn't doubt it.

Hok offered Ying a polite bow. "Safe travels, and good luck."

Ying nodded back. He let go of the pylon and the current began to pull him gently away. ShaoShu waved an enthusiastic goodbye, and Ying actually returned the wave. Then he turned away, grabbed the oar, and began to row downstream.

CHAPTER 25

The river was pleasantly smooth, and Ying felt himself relaxing as he left the crowded city behind. Five hours later, he spotted the pagodas.

Ying turned the skiff south, as the pet vendor had directed, and headed up a rather wide creek. He lifted the oar out of the water so that it wouldn't drag along the bottom, and picked up the push pole. He had to work against the creek's current, but it wasn't difficult. The current was light and his shoulder felt strong.

As Ying poled the boat forward, the landscape quickly changed from flat farmland along the Qiantang River to steep, ragged hillsides farther inland. The slopes were thick with evergreens, but some had hundreds of wide steps carved into them, where farmers grew crops of tea leaves all the way up to the hilltops. Ying had never seen anything like it. It seemed the locals were determined to squeeze a living out of this scenic but rugged landscape.

Ying took a deep breath of the fresh, warm air. It smelled of pine, cypress, and green tea. He felt oddly at home. He'd heard a saying once about this region: "Above is Heaven, below is Hangzhou." He had to agree.

A little more than one *li* up the creek, Ying reached his destination. It was exactly as the pet vendor had told him it would be.

The house looked very old, but solid as a mountain. It was single-story and fashioned from brown bricks. It had a traditional green-tiled roof, and each of the roof's corners swept sharply upward to dispel evil spirits. Standing guard at the end of each corner was an ornate stone dragon. Each dragon was different, and Ying couldn't seem to pull his eyes from them. They faced north, south, east, and west. Each also represented a different season. Whoever had carved them had put a lot of effort and energy into them. Ying could almost feel them pulsating with life.

Ying couldn't help but think about the dragon scrolls and the treasure. The scroll map did lead to this area, and a house like this one seemed to be an appropriate place to hide a dragon's hoard. He would have to keep his eyes open for potential clues.

Ying looked farther down the creek and saw a garden thick with early-autumn vegetables. In the center of it knelt a small woman wearing a large straw hat. In one hand, she held several clumps of weeds. In the other was a long blade used for digging them up. She turned and stared at Ying.

A deep chill ran down Ying's spine. The woman's face was shadowed by the wide-brimmed hat, but it didn't matter. He knew who she was.

Nervous tension twisted Ying's stomach muscles into knots. His limbs grew numb, and he felt the pole slipping out of his hands. He gripped it tighter and continued pushing the skiff up the creek.

Ying watched as his mother slowly stood and advanced toward him. She dropped the clumps of weeds at the garden's edge but kept the blade in her hand.

The black silk mask fluttered across Ying's face, and he began to fumble with it, cursing himself. Why was he acting like a nervous child? He needed to keep his head clear. After all, his mother was holding a weapon. Ying shook his head violently, flinging the mask from his face, and pushed the skiff ashore.

Ying's mother stopped several paces from the skiff and removed her hat. Physically, she looked the same as he remembered. Her eyes were large, her nose was small, and her lips were full. Her long black hair was pulled back in a braid and several wisps hung free around her cheeks.

Ying stared at his mother as though she were a stranger. He bowed. "Greetings. I am Ying."

His mother scanned the dragon creases carved into his face. He knew that she was looking right through them, into his soul. "So I see," she replied. "You have changed, my son."

"Yes, I have."

Ying's mother nodded. "Welcome, then, Ying. You may call me WanSow."

Ying blinked and thought, *Cloud Hand?* That wasn't her name. She'd changed it.

WanSow seemed to read his mind. "Like the seasons, many things change. You and me included. I am rather surprised you recognized me. You were very young when we last saw one another."

Ying gestured to his face. "I am surprised *you* recognized *me.*"

WanSow shook her head. "If I were blindfolded, I would know who you are. Your father's *chi* is strong in you."

Ying felt another chill run down his spine. He didn't reply.

"How did you find me?" WanSow asked.

"It's a long story," Ying said.

"Why have you come? You don't seem particularly happy to see me again."

"I came here for answers."

WanSow closed her eyes. "I may not have the answers you seek. Or, worse, you may not like the answers you hear."

"I'll take my chances."

WanSow opened her eyes. Ying thought he saw a glimmer of challenge in them.

"So, you're a risk taker?" she asked.

"I suppose I am," Ying replied. "Why?"

"Because if you are, you will be willing to take part in a simple exercise with me. If you accomplish the task, I will answer all of your questions. However, if you fail, you will stay and work with me until you can complete the task. Agreed?"

"No, I need more details," Ying said. "What is the task? And what is this work you are talking about if I fail? I must be back in Hangzhou in a few days."

WanSow flicked a wisp of long black hair out of her eyes. "If you fail, the work is a series of mental and physical drills to help you further develop and focus your *chi*. As for the task, all you have to do is attack me and push me over."

"What?"

"The exercises I practice build strength from the inside out. They help a person remain grounded on many levels. You would benefit from the training. I can tell."

Ying's eyes narrowed. "Why would I want to attack you?"

"Because I am challenging you. Are you afraid?"

Ying frowned. "No. What techniques can I use?"

"Any technique you may know."

Ying nodded. "Let's get this over with, then." He put his hands out. "How do we begin?"

"You decide. I'm just going to stand here."

Ying shrugged. He formed eagle-claw fists with both hands and walked up to his mother.

WanSow dropped the blade she had been holding

and sank into a deep horse stance. She raised her hands to chest height.

Ying thrust both his fists out at WanSow's shoulders. It wasn't a complicated attack. He expected his mother to shift sideways, but she didn't. Instead, she leaned backward, absorbing Ying's force, and latched on to his wrists with her hands.

Ying found himself being pulled off balance. He twisted to one side, expecting to draw away, but his mother twisted with him. His balance was now really off center, and just as Ying thought he might right himself, WanSow jerked his wrists hard in the direction he was leaning. She let go, and Ying tumbled to the ground.

WanSow straightened, her feet still firmly rooted to the ground. She took a few steps backward and winked at him.

Ying stood and scowled. He formed two eagle-claw fists again and ran straight at his mother. Again, she sank into a deep horse stance, raising her hands chest-high.

A moment before impact, Ying leaped into the air. He pulled his legs back and fired them out at WanSow's head.

WanSow ducked.

As Ying sailed over his mother's head, she reached up and grabbed the seat of his black silk pants. She latched on tight and twisted in the direction of Ying's momentum, pulling her body powerfully down toward the earth. Ying's trajectory changed and he found himself slammed to the ground, backside-first.

Ying groaned and turned to see WanSow's feet still rooted to the earth. She smiled at him. "How many chances do I get? I could do this all day."

Ying stood and dusted himself off. "Well, I can't."

"Are you planning to leave? Or are you going to keep your end of the deal and train with me?"

Ying frowned. "I'm going to keep my end of the deal, at least until I have to leave. Just make sure you keep *your* end."

"Of course," WanSow replied. "Feel free to try and accomplish your task anytime, any day. It is an important exercise in control to be ready at any given moment."

"I'll remember that," Ying said. "I should warn you, though, I am a very quick study."

"We shall see," WanSow said with a smirk. She looked up at the sky. "It will be dark soon. Come into the house. I suggest you get some rest. First thing tomorrow, your training begins."

CHAPTER 26

Ying woke early the next day, well before sunrise. He wanted some time alone before he began his training with his mother at daybreak. He put on his silk robe and pants but left his feet bare.

Ying slipped out of the house onto the cool, dew-drenched grass. A chill raced from the soles of his feet to the top of his head, making his scalp tingle. He savored it. It made him feel alive.

Ying rounded the back corner of the house and stopped dead in his tracks. Someone was outside, standing still as a statue. At least, that's what he thought at first. He soon realized that the person was actually moving incredibly slow. It was his mother.

Ying watched, hypnotized by how slowly she was

moving. Her belly—not her chest—rose and fell steadily with each breath, much like the elderly people he had seen along the canal. Her movements were light and flowing, yet somehow heavy and dense at the same time. Like a rain cloud.

Ying didn't know how long he stood watching her, but by the time his mother had finished, the sun was beginning to rise. She turned to him, seemingly in a trance. Then she blinked a few times, and Ying saw consciousness return to her eyes.

"Oh, good morning, Ying," WanSow said in a gentle voice. "I didn't see you there."

"I've been here quite some time," he replied.

"I was meditating," WanSow said. "That's what *Tai Chi Chuan* is, moving meditation."

"That's what you're going to teach me, *Tai Chi*?" Ying asked. "Is that what you used against me yesterday?"

WanSow nodded.

"I thought *Tai Chi* was a collection of movements and breathing exercises for old people."

"It is internal and external exercise for anyone of any age. Elderly individuals particularly enjoy it because a person doesn't have to be big and strong or young and flexible to do it. It also happens to be a very effective fighting art. *Tai Chi Chuan,* or *Tai Chi* for short, is many things. Are you ready to begin?"

"Shouldn't we eat breakfast first?"

"No. *Tai Chi* is best done the moment you wake up.

It gives you energy for the entire day. We will start with a breathing exercise."

"I already know how to breathe," Ying said.

WanSow frowned. "This is serious. Breathing is the key to controlling and increasing your *chi.*"

"If you say so," Ying said, rolling his eyes. "Teach me how to breathe. Maybe after that, you can teach me how to walk."

"Walking comes later," WanSow said. "After breathing, I will teach you how to stand. Now, do as I do. . . ."

Four hours later, Ying was still practicing just one breathing technique. He'd never been so bored in his life. They took a break for lunch, then spent the entire afternoon on just one standing posture. Ying was ready to pull his hair out.

By evening, Ying was certain he was going to lose his mind. He didn't have time for all this monotony. Tonglong was probably still on their tail, and Ying wasn't any closer to finding the treasure. This house still seemed like a logical place to hide it, so during his few training breaks he had poked around as much as possible, looking for clues. He found no sign of the treasure at all.

Ying went to bed early that night, more out of frustration than fatigue. He needed a plan to end this nonsense. He glanced around the room, looking for something that could help him. At the foot of the bed was an object that might just be his ticket out. It was a small trunk that stood about knee-high. That could work.

Ying made a mental note to stay in bed and pretend to oversleep so that his mother would come in and wake him. If he was lucky, by this time tomorrow he would be back in Hangzhou, his arms full of treasure.

CHAPTER 27

"There it is!" Charles announced. "Starboard side. The famous apothecary. Prepare to dock."

Malao looked to his left. "Where? I don't see it."

Charles shook his head. "How many times do I have to tell you, Malao? *Starboard* means 'right.' "

"Oh," Malao said.

Fu grabbed a rope and walked to the starboard side. "That building is huge. It's a medicine store?"

"Yes," Charles said. "An apothecary. I've never seen another one even close to this size. PawPaw was right—I'm sure Hok wouldn't be able to resist it."

"Where do we dock?" Malao asked.

"Wherever we can find a space," Charles replied. "There," he said, pointing to a small slip a few hundred paces upstream. "That will do nicely. All hands on deck!"

Fu uncoiled a section of his rope near the bow, and Malao hurried to do the same at the stern. Charles fought back a grin. Fu and Malao might have been landlubbers, but they were becoming surprisingly good sailors. Fu was incredibly strong and could lift things even Charles couldn't manage, while Malao was as happy as a clam up in the rigging, often swinging around at perilous heights for fun. Thanks to them, Charles was able to make it down the coast and to Hangzhou in record time.

Charles steered his boat into the slip and jumped ashore. Fu tossed him a line, and Charles tied off the bow. Malao threw his rope, and Charles tied off the stern. He motioned for Fu and Malao to come ashore, too.

Charles stepped away from the dock's edge and fought back another grin. They had been at sea almost two weeks without setting foot on dry land. It would be amusing to see what happened when Fu's and Malao's legs hit solid ground.

Malao leaped onto the dock first, landing in a low crouch. As soon as he stood up, he began to weave like a drunkard. He took a tentative step forward, then toppled over, giggling.

"What's gotten into you?" Fu grumbled from the boat.

Malao looked at him and kept giggling.

Fu rolled his eyes and climbed ashore. As he

straightened, Fu started to weave back and forth, too, his legs wobbling.

"What the—" Fu began to say.

"Sea legs," Charles said. "It will take a few hours for you to get used to solid ground again. By tomorrow morning, you'll be back to your old self."

Fu stepped forward hesitantly and growled, "I don't like this."

Malao giggled some more and stood. He took several steps forward, wobbling exaggeratedly. "I do," he said.

"It figures," Fu replied.

"That's enough fun for now," Charles said. "Let's go inside."

Fu sniffed the air. "Wait, I smell chicken cooking. I hope the apothecary has a food stand."

Charles shook his head. He reached into the pouch tied to his sash and handed Fu a few coins, then pointed upstream. "I believe the food stand is that way. It's not too far. Get whatever you'd like, and bring me something, too. Fish balls on a stick, if they have some."

Malao made a sour face. "Fish balls?"

Charles sighed. "Balls of fish meat, marinated in soy sauce and cooked on a grill. They are quite tasty. You should try some." He pointed to the apothecary. "I'm going in there to see if I can learn any news about Hok. Meet me inside."

"Okay," Malao said. He walked away with Fu at his side, both of them weaving like flags in the wind.

Charles headed for the apothecary. He stepped through a pair of enormous red doors, and his senses were immediately assaulted by a complex combination of sights, sounds, and smells. The air was thick with a spiced perfume made from a thousand different herbs that had been dried, ground, and mixed into a hundred thousand combinations. He heard people talking loudly in different languages, discussing treatments for everything from sour stomachs to headaches to bed-wetting. Barrels and other containers of every size and color were stacked to the ceiling, forming narrow walkways that meandered through the building like tracks left by a dizzy snake. It was almost overwhelming.

Charles got his bearings and headed into the maze of aisles in search of a shopkeeper. He tried his best to remember the way back to the front door.

After innumerable twists and turns, Charles spotted someone who might be in charge. He was an older man with thinning gray hair, and he stood behind the longest counter Charles had ever seen. The man was gingerly taking small terra-cotta bottles out from under the counter and placing them on the countertop for a customer to inspect.

Charles watched the customer carefully pull a stopper out of one of the bottles and adjust an extraordinarily long ponytail braid. Charles stared at the man's clothes. He was wearing a soldier's uniform. It was Tonglong.

Charles turned to hurry away when he heard

Tonglong speak. Charles only caught one word, but it was enough to make him start creeping back toward Tonglong to see if he could hear more. That word was "Hok."

"So, you haven't seen a pale girl with brown hair, or a teenage boy with his face carved to resemble a dragon?" Tonglong asked the older man.

The man, who Charles was now certain was the shopkeeper, shook his head. "No, sir."

"You will send someone for me if you do see either of them, right?" Tonglong asked.

"Immediately," the shopkeeper said. "Will you be in Hangzhou long?"

"As long as it takes to find them."

"If you don't mind my asking, a man of your rank has traveled all this way to find two children?"

"They are special children," Tonglong said. "They have something I want. So, it seems, do you." He gestured to the numerous bottles on the counter. "I will take them all."

Charles watched the shopkeeper's eyes widen. "What on earth could you possibly do with so much snake venom?"

Tonglong chuckled. "It's not for me. It's a gift. For my mother. She couldn't make the trip here with me, so I thought I might bring her back a little something."

"Snake venom?" the shopkeeper asked.

"My mother has an interesting . . . hobby," Tonglong said with a grin. "Wrap these up for me."

"Oh, I'm sorry," the shopkeeper said. "You will have

to carry these bottles individually. Packaging them is too risky. The stoppers could pop out or the bottles could break. I've seen these things happen before with snake venom. People have lost their lives. I am sorry."

"I will carry them individually, then," Tonglong said. "I plan to return tomorrow to do some more shopping. I will pay you then."

"As you wish, General," the shopkeeper said.

Charles had hoped to hear more about what Tonglong was up to, but it seemed his conversation with the shopkeeper was drawing to a close. It was time to leave.

As Tonglong began to carefully pick up the small bottles, Charles headed for the door. He'd taken three steps when he heard Tonglong shout, "Hey, you! Round Eye! Step over here."

Charles began to run. He raced back through the maze, knocking items and customers to the floor. Tonglong called out, "To the front door, men! There is a young round eye coming your way. Stop him!"

Charles reached the front door without seeing a single soldier. He grinned and rushed out of the doorway, directly into the arms of two very large men. Soldiers.

Charles writhed and twisted and kicked, but it was no use. He soon gave up. Tonglong came out with his arms full of snake-venom bottles. "Take him to the barracks," Tonglong said. "I will go on ahead. As you can imagine, the last thing I want to do is drop one of these on myself—or on you."

"Yes, sir!" the soldiers said in unison.

Tonglong nodded to them and walked away. Charles watched, dejected, as Tonglong hurried along the riverbank, then turned away from the water and headed up a narrow side street.

"Let's go," one of the soldiers said, and both burly men began to drag Charles in the same direction Tonglong had gone. Charles looked back at the apothecary's entrance and saw people streaming out as fast as their legs would carry them. They were obviously worried about the soldiers, too.

Charles glanced upstream, and his heart leaped. Fu and Malao were strolling along the riverfront on wobbly legs, both intently focused on consuming their dinners.

"Fu! Malao!" Charles shouted. "Help!"

Fu and Malao looked up and came running. Malao held a skewer of fish balls in each hand, while Fu held the remains of a chicken carcass. Fu roared and hurled the carcass at the head of the soldier to Charles' right. The man ducked forward and Charles lifted his knee, driving it hard into the soldier's face.

The soldier howled and straightened, and Fu rushed forward, slamming a meaty fist into the man's Adam's apple. The man choked, and Fu hit him again on the side of the neck with his forearm. The soldier went down.

Malao stopped in front of the second soldier and shrieked loudly. He whipped the skewers forward with a quick snap of his wrists, flinging fish balls into the man's face. The soldier closed his eyes for a moment, and Malao dropped low, jamming the pointed bamboo skewers into the man's thighs.

The soldier screamed and his legs buckled, and Charles broke free. As the man teetered forward, Charles threw an uppercut into his jaw. The soldier's head rocked back and he toppled to the ground, unconscious.

Charles looked around for Tonglong. He wasn't there. He must not have heard the ruckus.

"Let's get out of here!" Malao said.

Charles nodded. "Follow me." He took a step toward his sloop and heard a shrill whistle behind him. It sounded like a large bird.

Fu released a questioning growl. "Hok?"

Charles snapped his head around. Hok was standing alone in the apothecary doorway.

"Hok! Hok! Hok!" Malao squealed in a hushed tone. He raced toward her.

"In here," Hok said.

Charles and Fu ran after Malao, and all three of them followed Hok through the apothecary entrance, into the maze of aisles. There wasn't a single customer left in the store. They made it to a back storage room and Hok led them inside. She gestured for them to sit at a large table covered with candles, then locked the door behind them.

"We'll be safe in here for a little while," Hok said as she sat down. "But we shouldn't press our luck. The shopkeeper is a very nice man, obviously. I don't want to get him in trouble."

Charles stared at her, dumbfounded. "You work here?"

"*Volunteer* is a better word," Hok replied. "I happened to mention PawPaw when I first spoke with him, and he got very excited. It seems they are old friends."

"PawPaw is the reason we're here, too," Charles said. "How long have you been here?"

"We arrived in Hangzhou yesterday."

"You and Ying?" Fu asked.

Hok nodded. "And a small boy called ShaoShu."

Fu growled.

"Where are they now?" Charles asked.

"Ying is several *li* down the river," Hok said. She glanced quickly around the room. "I don't know where ShaoShu is. He could be hiding, or he could have wandered off to explore. I've learned he likes to do both."

"What do you do here?" Malao asked.

"Grind herbs, mix tonics—lots of things. I needed something to keep me busy while I waited for Ying to return, and this is fun for me."

"When is Ying coming back?" Charles asked.

"ShaoShu and I were supposed to meet him in front of the apothecary at sunset tomorrow," Hok said. "Unfortunately, there is no way we can do that now. Not with Tonglong and his men here."

"Why don't we go to Ying?" Charles suggested. "We can't stay here, anyway. Do you know where he is?"

"I know where he was supposed to go," Hok said, "but I won't be surprised if he is no longer there."

“Where did he go?” Malao asked.

“To meet his mother.”

The room fell silent.

“See,” Hok said. “That’s what I mean. There is no telling what might have happened.”

“Well, we have to do something,” Charles said. “Let’s just go there now and take our chances.”

Hok rubbed the back of her neck. “Maybe you’re right, Charles. Maybe we should go. But we can’t leave right now. I don’t want to abandon ShaoShu.”

Charles nodded. “Let’s give him until tomorrow morning. If he shows up, then we take him with us. If not, we leave without him and come back some other time. What do all of you think?”

“It makes sense,” Malao said.

“To me, too,” Fu replied.

Hok waited a long moment, then nodded. “Okay, let’s handle it that way. I’m staying at a nearby inn with ShaoShu, and the room is very big. We can all go there and wait until morning. Maybe ShaoShu will even show up. I think we will be safe there. The shopkeeper owns the inn, too.” She turned to Charles. “What about your boat? Will it be safe until tomorrow?”

“It will be fine,” Charles said. “I’m docked alongside hundreds of other foreign boats. No one will connect it to me or any of you. We will have to be sneaky getting aboard if we wait until morning, though. Simple disguises should work. I’ve done it many times. I tend to stand out in a crowd, you know.”

“Me too,” Hok said, and gave Charles a satisfied nod.

“Anything else?” Charles asked the group.

No one replied.

“Then there is nothing left to discuss,” Charles said. “Tonight, we wait. Tomorrow morning—at the latest—we set sail.”

CHAPTER 28

Ying woke just before sunrise with tired eyes and a heavy head. While he'd begun the night sleeping just fine, he'd ended it with troublesome dreams of being watched. He slipped out of bed and peered out the window.

His mother was already outside, practicing in the early-morning moonlight. Perhaps she had been out there for a long while and disturbed his sleep. Or maybe she had come in and spied on him? He'd dreamed that he'd heard noises, too. Not that it mattered. He was leaving today with what he needed. She wouldn't have learned anything last night that would stop him.

Ying crawled back into bed to wait.

A quarter of an hour after sunrise, WanSow entered his room. Ying's eyes were closed, and he kept his breathing slow and steady—ironically, just as she had taught him the previous morning.

"Rise and shine," WanSow said as she stepped up to his bed. "Time to get back to your training."

Ying opened his eyes and faked a yawn, which wasn't all that difficult to do.

"You look exhausted," WanSow said. "Perhaps you should sleep some more."

"I'm fine," Ying said. He sat up and swung his legs over the side of the bed. He was fully dressed in his black silk robe and pants.

WanSow took a step back. "I see that you are all ready to go. I will meet you outside."

"Wait," Ying said. He stood and leaned toward her. "I want to show you something."

WanSow took another step back. Ying was invading her personal space.

"Why don't you show me outside?" WanSow said. "There isn't much room in here."

"It will only take a moment," Ying said. He took a step forward.

WanSow took a third step back, and Ying heard her heel bump into the trunk at the foot of his bed. He lunged toward her, thrusting both of his palms into her shoulders.

WanSow wilted like a flower, her upper body absorbing much of the impact. However, her knee buckled against the trunk, and she toppled over.

WanSow looked up at Ying from the floor, a look of disgust on her face. "Tripping me over the trunk was not an honorable attack. A dragon would never have done that."

"Not even a vengeful dragon?" Ying asked.

WanSow's eyes narrowed. "Your father gave you that name, not me."

Ying shrugged. "It doesn't matter anymore. My name is Ying now."

"So it is," WanSow said. She pushed herself to her feet. "What is it you want to know, Ying?"

"Grandmaster had a collection of secret dragon scrolls that he stole from my father. One of them had a sketch of the human body on each side. Do you know anything about it?"

WanSow frowned. "You can ask me anything you'd like and the first thing you want to know about is a treasure map?"

"You do know about it," Ying said.

"I do," WanSow replied. "But what makes you think Grandmaster stole it and the other scrolls from your father?"

"I saw him do it. I might have only been a toddler, but I remember. He took them right after he killed my father."

WanSow shook her head and sat down on Ying's bed. "You saw Grandmaster taking back what was rightfully his. Those scrolls had been in his family for many generations. Your father was the real thief. He'd stolen them from Grandmaster."

"What?" Ying said. "You're lying."

"Why would I lie about this?"

Ying didn't have an answer.

"Ying, what do you know about your father?"

"I . . . I don't know," Ying said hesitantly. "Not much, I suppose."

"Well, your father was not a nice man. In fact, he was a very bad man."

Ying swallowed hard.

"Your father led a band of cutthroat thieves. They stole indiscriminately, often harming innocent people. Grandmaster had had enough of their deplorable actions. More than that, he'd had enough of his oldest son damaging the family's reputation—"

"Oldest son?" Ying interrupted. "What are you talking about?"

WanSow's large eyes widened. "Oh, my. You don't know, do you?"

"Know what?"

"The relationship between your father and Grandmaster?"

Ying shook his head. "Wait . . . you mean—"

WanSow lowered her head. "Grandmaster was your father's father. I'm sorry. I thought you knew. I'd always assumed Grandmaster would tell you."

Ying sat on the bed next to his mother. He was beginning to feel dizzy. "So, Grandmaster was my . . . grandfather?"

WanSow laid a hand on his shoulder. "Yes. But you keep talking about Grandmaster in the past tense. Has something happened to him?"

"You haven't heard?" Ying asked.

"I don't hear much these days," WanSow said. "We are quite a long way from Cangzhen, and I am no longer part of any network."

"Grandmaster's dead," Ying said.

"What happened?"

Ying looked away. "I killed him."

WanSow lowered her head again. "Oh, dear."

"If I had known he was my grandfather—" Ying began.

"What's done is done," WanSow said, raising her head. "Past is past. All that matters now is what you do in the future." She looked at him. "What is it you plan to do, Ying?"

Ying straightened. "I don't know now. I need to think about some things. I had planned to find the dragon scroll treasure."

"I see," WanSow said. "I suppose it is rightfully yours. The treasure and the map have been in your family for hundreds of years. May I ask what you plan to do with the treasure?"

"I don't know yet."

"But you want it nonetheless?"

"Yes."

"Then you shall have it," WanSow said. "Whenever you might be ready. I should warn you, though, your family was selected to keep watch over the treasure, not take it."

Ying paused. "I know the legend. I never dreamed that I might be a member of the keeper family, though."

"Think about your responsibilities," WanSow said. "The treasure is real. Whether it was put there by a dragon is up for debate. A person's position on this matter depends on how superstitious he or she is."

Ying nodded.

"This house is yours, too," WanSow said. "Along with much of the surrounding land. It, too, has been in your family for generations."

Ying didn't know what to say. He glanced around as if seeing this house for the first time. It was old and solid, as Grandmaster had been. "How long have you been living here?"

"I came soon after you and I separated. Grandmaster suggested I come. Cangzhen had already become his new home. He wanted me to help keep the family secrets."

"Secrets?" Ying said.

WanSow nodded. "Like the treasure. I take it you have seen the dragon scroll map?"

"Seen it?" Ying said. "I memorized it."

"Then you know that it leads to this general area."

"Yes."

"Well, anybody clever enough to read that map and follow it here was supposed to be clever enough to find this house. I'm sure you noticed the dragons on the roof."

Ying nodded. "Do they hold clues?"

"Yes," WanSow replied. "That was a wise assumption. The clues lead to a second map etched in a cave far behind the house, and I'll show it to you. But first I'd like to ask you a question, if you don't mind."

"What?" Ying asked.

"The dragon scroll map explains how you found your way to this house, but you didn't seem at all surprised to find me here. Why not?"

"I learned about you from a pet vendor in Xuzhou," Ying said. "I acquired some dragon bone from him."

"Was he a grizzled old man with horribly scarred hands?"

"Yes."

WanSow nodded. "He used to be part of your father's camp."

"I know."

"He worked here in Hangzhou for many years, too," WanSow said. "I should never have told him my whereabouts." She paused. "Is there any chance he told anyone else about this place?"

Ying opened his mouth to reply, but someone else spoke up from outside the bedroom window.

"What an excellent question!" the voice proclaimed. "I think I can answer that one. Yes! And now I know about the second treasure map, too. Thank you. Don't worry about the pet vendor sharing your secrets, dear lady. He won't be telling anyone anything, ever again."

Ying turned toward the open window and saw

Tonglong's head rise up in front of it. Tonglong shoved the barrel of a short *qiang* through it and said, "Don't even think of attacking. My men have the house surrounded. If I go down, Ying, so will you and your mother."

WanSow smirked. "If anything happens to me, you will never find the treasure."

"That's not true," Tonglong said. "And you know it. It might take my men several days to find the cave without your help, but we will find it eventually. Better that you work with me now."

Ying's upper lip curled back, but he didn't speak.

Tonglong turned to him. "What's gotten into you? The Ying I knew would be spitting threats left and right. Then again, I suppose learning you'd killed your own grandfather might shut anybody up." He laughed and pointed the *qiang* at WanSow. "Take me to the cave."

Ying watched his mother's shoulders slump as she stood and walked out of the house. He followed close on her heels. Ying was hopeful that he might get a chance to attack Tonglong, but his hopes were upset the moment he stepped outside. More than twenty soldiers encircled the house. They had been quite some distance away but closed in quickly. Each one held a long *qiang* raised in either his direction or his mother's.

Ying glanced at his mother. She shrugged as if to say, *There is nothing we can do.*

WanSow led them around the garden in which he'd

first seen her and up a steep grade thick with pine trees. Ying walked behind her, while Tonglong followed Ying just out of striking distance, his *qiang* aimed at the center of Ying's back. Fifteen soldiers followed Tonglong, and the other five soldiers ransacked the house.

Ying heard a shriek overhead and looked up to see an eagle soaring above them. He shook his head at the irony.

"What's next, Ying?" Tonglong asked. "A tiger cub? A white monkey?" He laughed. "You know, those former brothers of yours and a round eye attacked two of my men in Hangzhou yesterday. In some ways, you have them to thank for my coming this morning. I assumed that you were with them and that you were all heading to this dragon house immediately. I worked through the night to hire a boat and crew large enough to transport my twenty best men and the treasure we're about to take."

Ying said nothing.

They made it to the top of the steep hill, then slid and scraped their way down the other side. They repeated this two more times over progressively taller, steeper hills until Ying guessed that they had traveled well over a *li*.

Halfway up the fourth hill, in an area thick with foliage, the ground suddenly leveled off. WanSow pushed aside a wall of ferns to reveal a small cave entrance. It was about as wide as Ying's shoulders and as tall as his chest.

"Okay, so this would have taken a few weeks to locate," Tonglong said. "This had better not be a trick."

WanSow ignored Tonglong. She ducked into the cave and Ying went in after her, followed by Tonglong with his short *qiang*. The soldiers waited just outside the entrance.

Once inside, Ying found he could stand without difficulty. The cave was dark, and he could just make out his mother crossing to the back corner. She hunched down, low to the ground, and Ying heard the *clink* of metal hitting stone. He headed toward her and realized that she was striking a fire stone with a piece of metal. A few sparks found their mark, and a small candle ignited.

Ying wondered if his mother had hidden a *qiang* or a knife in that corner along with the candles and fire-starting items.

She hadn't.

WanSow used the little candle to light a second small candle, which she handed to Ying. He raised it over his head and saw the true dimensions of the space. It wasn't very big, roughly twenty paces wide and thirty paces long. He watched his mother move to the back wall and stop there, facing it.

Ying walked to her side and saw that she was staring at a huge section of rock face that had been ground flat and polished to a high sheen. A simple map had been carved into it. Ying memorized the map in three heartbeats.

Tonglong approached and stared over WanSow's

shoulder from several paces behind. It took him much longer to commit the map to memory.

Tonglong backed up to the entrance, leaving Ying and his mother alone in front of the map. "Who carved that?" Tonglong asked.

"No one knows," WanSow replied.

"According to the legends, it was China's mystical Treasure Dragon," Tonglong said. "Do you believe that?"

"I have no reason to disbelieve it," WanSow said. "Why do you ask?"

Tonglong smiled. "I was just wondering if I need to keep one eye fixed over my shoulder after I take his treasure. I've been told certain dragons can be vengeful creatures." He looked at Ying and laughed, then pointed his *qiang* at Ying's head.

Something inside Ying snapped. He threw his candle at Tonglong and leaped forward as if he had nothing left to lose, for indeed that was the case. He heard the *click* as the hammer on Tonglong's *qiang* fell, and in the same moment he saw a flash of metal strike Tonglong in the side of the head. His mother had thrown the fire stone's strike bar. Tonglong cried out, twisting the *qiang* in her direction.

Fizz . . . BANG!

Tonglong's *qiang* erupted with a deafening *BOOM!* inside the small cave. His shot went high, over WanSow's head, and was followed by the terrible rumbling sound of massive boulders shifting. WanSow managed to take two steps toward the cave's entrance before a huge section of the ceiling collapsed directly above her.

"No!" Ying shouted. He stopped short of Tonglong and turned toward the pile of rubble that had buried his mother. Out of the corner of his eye, Ying saw Tonglong drop the smoking *qiang* and leap backward out of the entrance as another wave of grinding and shifting shuddered around them. Ying scrambled for the entrance but was too slow. A second avalanche of debris fell, this time over the entrance. In the blink of an eye, the opening was filled in with more rock than Ying could hope to move in a year. He was thrust into absolute darkness.

Ying glanced around for his mother's candle. It had been snuffed out. He could hardly breathe. Chalky dust filled his mouth, nose, ears, and eyes. He coughed and called out to his mother.

She didn't reply.

Ying clawed his way around the cave, searching over, under, and in between jagged piles of stone until his fingers finally found something soft. It was his mother's arm. Ying fumbled as quickly as he dared with rocks of all sizes, tossing them aside, digging his mother free.

But it was no use.

After moving everything he could in the blackness, Ying realized that his mother's chest and waist were wedged beneath a boulder as big as a horse. He would never be able to lift it alone.

Hesitantly, Ying took his mother's arm in his

hands, dreading what he knew he had to do next. He placed his battered fingertips on her wrist and felt for a pulse.

He felt nothing.

For the first time since he'd lost his best friend, Luk, Ying felt tears welling up in his eyes.

CHAPTER 29

Darkness enveloped Ying. He dropped his head, his mother's arm still in his hands. He felt as helpless as a toddler.

"I am so sorry, Mother," Ying whispered. "So very sorry. I wish there was something I could do to help you. . . ."

Ying felt a twitch beneath his fingertips, and he nearly cried out in surprise. Was that a pulse? He concentrated hard and noticed that, yes, there was definitely something there, beating delicately, slowly, until it started to grow stronger and stronger.

Miraculously, just a few moments later, WanSow began to speak. Her words were faint but audible. Ying realized that she had slowed her heart rate to cause herself to slip into unconsciousness. Her heartbeat had been so slow that he couldn't feel it. Now she was bringing herself back.

"You can still help me," WanSow whispered. "You can help us all. Stop Tonglong." She coughed. "Go."

"Go where?" Ying asked, his eyes darting futilely around the utter blackness. "The entrance is blocked. I don't even know where it is anymore."

"There is a way out," WanSow whispered. "Feel your way over to the smooth stone map and push on the right side with all your strength. It should swing outward like a door. There is a passageway beyond. A natural tunnel. It leads outside." She coughed again. "I watched the rocks as they fell. The map should be unobstructed."

"I can't leave you like this," Ying said.

"Yes, you can," WanSow whispered. "Listen to me. I am slowing my heart rate down again. I will soon slip back into unconsciousness. I will feel no pain. I believe I can survive like this for a day and a night. Perhaps two nights. Stop Tonglong first, then return and help me if there is time. Goodbye, my son."

Before Ying could say a word, his mother slipped into a deep meditative state.

Ying ground his teeth. Tonglong was going to pay. He bowed farewell to his mother and began to fumble around for the stone map. It didn't take long to find, and it took even less time to open.

An hour later, Ying was back at the ransacked house. *His* ransacked house. Tonglong and the soldiers were gone. Ying began to look frantically for the skiff, and when he finally did find it, he shrieked in frustration. Tonglong's men had sunk it in the creek. He would have to head back on foot.

It was slow going, trying to run along the creek bank. There were many more twists and turns than Ying remembered. Also, the rocks on the shore were covered with thick algae and slime. Another hour passed before he reached the twin pagodas where the creek met the river. Ying turned to walk upstream and jumped as someone called out his name.

"Ying! Ying! Over here!" a girl shouted.

It was Hok. She was in a small sailing vessel with Charles, Fu, and Malao. Charles steered the boat toward the shore and yelled, "Swim out toward the center of the river, Ying! We'll pick you up!"

Ying jumped in. The river was colder than he'd expected. He caught his breath and swam hard across the current. Charles swung the boat near, and Hok tossed Ying a line. Ying grabbed hold of it and hauled himself aboard.

"Th-th-thank you," Ying said to Hok.

Hok nodded. "You are welcome. Are you okay?"

Ying began to shiver uncontrollably. Whether it was a result of the cold water or stress, he wasn't sure. He glanced around the boat. "I'm fine. Where is ShaoShu?"

"I don't know," Hok said. "He wandered off somewhere and hadn't returned by the time we needed to leave. We will go back for him soon."

“We will have to go back for someone else, too,” Ying said. “My mother has been badly injured.”

“What happened?” Hok asked.

“Tonglong happened,” Ying said. “He is here.”

“We know,” Charles said. “Hok wanted to come here and warn you. I take it you’ve seen him?”

“Yes,” Ying replied. He looked at Hok. “There is a second map. Tonglong has seen it. We have to get to the treasure before they do.”

“How are we supposed to know where to go?” Fu growled.

Ying tapped the side of his head with a jittery finger. “I saw the m-m-map, too, Pussycat.” Ying began to glance up and down the riverbanks.

“What are you looking for?” Malao asked.

“Our location in relation to the map,” Ying replied. He pointed downstream, toward the sea. “We need to go that way. The treasure is hidden in a small cove on the coast.”

“Aye, aye,” Charles said. “Is the cove far?”

“I’m not sure of the map’s scale,” Ying replied. “How far is it to the sea?”

“Only about half an hour.”

“Then the treasure is quite close. Perhaps two hours south of the point where the river meets the sea.”

“How far ahead of us is Tonglong?” Charles asked.

Ying stopped to think. “I’m not sure exactly, but I would guess perhaps two hours.”

“I’ll do what I can to catch up with them,” Charles said. “We’re overloaded, but we’re not at risk of sinking. This sloop overloaded is still faster than any other craft her size."

Ying nodded and glanced around for a blanket or a tarp to help him get warm. Hok was one step ahead of him. She pulled a blanket from a storage bin in the bow and handed it to Ying.

"Thank you," Ying said.

Hok nodded and hurried off to attend to something with one of the sails. Ying closed his eyes and tried to relax.

Charles' sleek vessel raced down the river with amazing speed. Ying would have been exhilarated if he hadn't been so preoccupied with thoughts of his mother and their situation, not to mention Grandmaster.

They reached the end of the river in no time and spilled into the open sea. Charles' sloop seemed to take on a life of its own here. It rode the waves like a playful dragon, slicing smoothly through the whitecaps as it raced south with Charles standing strong at the helm.

An hour later, Ying's shaking finally subsided. An hour after that, he could sense that they were getting close. He felt it in his bones.

Charles looked at him and shouted over the roar of the waves, "We're almost there, aren't we?"

"I believe so," Ying shouted back.

"What are we looking for?" Charles asked.

"A hidden cave within a small cove," Ying said. "On the map, it was little more than an indentation on the edge of a tiny beach."

"It is probably well hidden," Charles said. "More than likely, it is flooded by the tide and impossible to find unless you know exactly where to look. Hiding valuables in a cave like that is an old pirate's trick."

Great, Ying thought. *More caves.* "Do you think it is flooded now?" he asked.

Charles stared at the shore for a moment, then shook his head. "The tide is coming in, but it's still fairly low. Look at the high-water marks on the rocks."

Ying looked at the rocks and understood. He scanned the area for signs of Tonglong but saw nothing. There weren't any other boats in sight.

They rounded a bend in the coast, and Ying saw a narrow opening in the rocks far ahead. Charles noticed it, too.

"There!" Charles said, pointing. "That hole looks promising."

"I think that's it," Ying replied. "All we need to do is—"

A Chinese junk suddenly slipped through the hole into the open sea. It was quite some distance away, but Ying could tell that it was large.

"Tonglong!" Charles said. "That has got to be him."

Ying slammed his fist into his palm.

Hok hurried over to Ying's side. "Are we too late?" she asked.

"I think so," Ying hissed.

Malao scurried up to the top of the sloop's tall mast for a better view, while Fu ran to the bow, his eyes focused intently on the junk. "I think I see Tonglong on deck," Fu said.

"I think so, too," Malao said. "But my eyes aren't as good as Fu's. The boat is pretty far away."

"Just a moment," Charles said. He opened a small hatch beneath the sloop's steering wheel and removed a spyglass. "I forgot about this. I took it from HaMo back on the Yellow River." He held the glass up to one eye and steered the boat with his hip.

"What do you see?" Ying asked.

"There are several soldiers on deck," Charles said, "and there appear to be several piles of treasure. Wait . . . I see Tonglong! He is holding a large white sword."

"We *are* too late!" Ying said, swearing. "Can we catch them?"

Charles lowered the spyglass and frowned. "I don't know. We have a lot of weight in this boat right now. I think we're out of luck."

"Let's try," Ying said.

Charles paused and shook his head. "No. They have a deck full of soldiers, and most of them are carrying *qiang*s. I also saw several cannons on deck. They would shred this sloop to pieces, and us along with it."

"Do you think they can see us?" Hok asked.

"If we can see them, they can see us," Charles said. "However, I didn't see anyone on their deck with a spyglass. I suppose it's just a matter of time before someone picks one up."

“What are our options, then?” Ying asked.

“We could disguise ourselves as best we can and follow them from a safe distance, out of cannon range,” Charles said. “They might stay on the water for days or even weeks, though.”

Ying thought about his mother, pinned inside the cave. He didn’t have that kind of time.

Ying pointed to the spyglass. “Let me see that.”

Charles handed the glass to Ying, and Ying raised it to his eye. He scanned the junk’s deck and saw the armed soldiers and the piles of treasure, just as Charles had said. Tonglong was there, too, standing beside a soldier. They were examining the large white sword. Three more white swords and a suit of flexible white armor lay at Tonglong’s feet.

Ying spat. He was about to put the spyglass down when he noticed something move behind the largest of the treasure piles. It was small and fast and darted underneath an old tarp the moment Tonglong bent down to pick up a different sword.

Ying burst out laughing and lowered the spyglass. He slapped Charles on the back. “Perhaps we still have a little luck left!”

“What is it?” Hok asked. “What did you see?”

“Not *what,*” Ying said. “*Who.*”

He handed the spyglass to Hok.

“It’s ShaoShu.”

THE FIVE ANCESTORS
adventures continue in
Book 6 . . .

Mouse

Jeff Stone lives in the Midwest with his wife and two children and practices the martial arts daily. He has worked as a photographer, an editor, a maintenance man, a technical writer, a ballroom dance instructor, a concert promoter, and a marketing director for companies that design schools, libraries, and skateboard parks. He began searching for his birth mother when he was eighteen and found her fifteen years later. He has subsequently found his birth father as well. He recently traveled to the Shaolin Temple in China and while there passed his black-belt test in Shaolin-do kung fu.